"What are you

"Preparing to kiss you."

"You have to prepare?"

Lucan's low chuckle sent waves of passion flowing through her blood.

"To do it right."

His hand closed around her back. He drew her in slowly, giving her time to change her mind.

As if.

He crushed her against the hardness of his body and took possession of her mouth. She was moaning deep in her throat as she mashed herself against him, trying to get closer. She ran her hands over his back, tangling in the softness of his still damp hair. She could feel the hard thrust of him as their bodies sought a closeness barred by clothing.

He pulled her head gently against his shoulder, stroking her hair then cupping the back of her head. "I don't want to hurt you and I'm losing control."

His voice was rough, thick with need. She smiled against his sweatshirt and lifted her face. "You won't hurt me. You would never hurt me."

DANI SINCLAIR

POLICE PROTECTOR

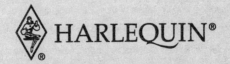

HARLEQUIN®

TORONTO • NEW YORK • LONDON
AMSTERDAM • PARIS • SYDNEY • HAMBURG
STOCKHOLM • ATHENS • TOKYO • MILAN • MADRID
PRAGUE • WARSAW • BUDAPEST • AUCKLAND

For my mother, Ruth Ann, who shares much in common
with Maureen O'Shay, including a deep love of family.

And for Roger, Chip, Dan and Barb as always

Recycling programs
for this product may
not exist in your area.

ISBN-13: 978-0-373-69445-7

POLICE PROTECTOR

Copyright © 2009 by Patricia A. Gagne

www.eHarlequin.com

Printed in U.S.A.

ABOUT THE AUTHOR

An avid reader, Dani Sinclair didn't discover romance novels until her mother loaned her one when she'd come for a visit. Dani's been hooked on the genre ever since, but she didn't take up writing seriously until her two sons were grown. With the premiere of *Mystery Baby* for Harlequin Intrigue in 1996, Dani's kept her computer busy ever since. She's a two-time RITA® Award finalist, for *Better Watch Out* in 1998 and *Midnight Prince* in 2008. Dani lives outside Washington, D.C., a place she's found to be a great source for both intrigue and humor!

You can write to her in care of the Harlequin Reader Service.

Books by Dani Sinclair

HARLEQUIN INTRIGUE
827—SECRET CINDERELLA
854—D.B. HAYES, DETECTIVE
870—RETURN TO STONY RIDGE
935—BEAUTIFUL BEAST
970—SLEEPING BEAUTY SUSPECT
1003—MIDNIGHT PRINCE
1084—BODYGUARD TO THE BRIDE
1104—THE MISSING MILLIONAIRE
1178—POLICE PROTECTOR

CAST OF CHARACTERS

Lucan O'Shay—The detective has been working overtime to catch a gang of thieves. Now he has to find a kid who's running around with hundred dollar bills in his backpack.

Kyra Wolfstead—She knew something was wrong at her sister's, but she never expected to drive into town and find her eight-year-old nephew being arrested on the street.

Kip Bowman—The eight-year-old has his younger siblings, Brian and Maggie, to protect. He intends to do just that, no matter what.

Casey Fillmont—Kyra's older sister is missing and her house has been ransacked. Her new husband, Jordan, and her ex are missing, as well.

Jordan Fillmont—Everyone claims to like the personable man who worked in the pro shop at the Oak Forest Country Club. So where is he?

Milt Bowman—Casey's ex-husband is a nice guy...until he starts drinking.

Louis Ventner—The general manager at Oak Forest Country Club is concerned about his missing employee.

Ralph Montgomery—Ventner's assistant doesn't like all the police attention the club is generating.

Bobby Krinegolt—The country club's gofer sees everything that goes on.

Maureen O'Shay—Lucan's mother is happy to take three children and their aunt under her wing.

Simon Testier—Kyra's ex-boyfriend won't take no for an answer.

Chapter One

Christmas carols played on the overhead speakers as Lucan O'Shay stepped to one side of the drink dispenser. He watched a young boy move down the aisle of the local convenience store. No one in the busy store paid any attention to the dark-haired boy with the green backpack.

The kid couldn't have been more than eight or nine years old, and he looked as if he hadn't bathed or changed his clothes in days. His jeans were of good quality, but stained and rumpled. It appeared as if he'd slept in his winter coat, and his hair and skin were badly in need of soap and water. He was thin, though not overly skinny. In fact there was nothing remarkable about the boy except for the furtive way his eyes darted about the area around him, as if he were afraid.

Lucan tensed as the boy picked up a bag of cookies, a box of cereal and a jar of peanut butter. All disappeared into the backpack at his feet so smoothly that even watching him, Lucan had to blink. The kid moved on, effortlessly adding a small container of milk and a bag of potato chips and carefully selecting three chocolate Santas and a box of candy canes.

Stealing? But the manager had said—

Before Lucan could shift position, the boy was in line at the register behind a sweaty construction worker. He was careful not to meet anyone's eyes. Lucan waited to see what the boy would do. Behind the counter, Salman's gaze met Lucan's. The manager inclined his head as the boy very carefully pulled each item from his backpack and set it on the counter.

Salman was outgoing and friendly with all his customers, but his efforts to make conversation with the boy netted him only a shake of the kid's head or a shrug. The boy wouldn't look at him.

"No bag." His voice betrayed his nerves, as did the way he shifted from foot to foot. Obviously, he wanted to pay and leave as quickly as possible.

Salman returned each item to the backpack. Even though he'd told Lucan what to expect, Lucan's jaw dropped as the boy pulled out what appeared to be an amazing wad of bills from the deep pocket of his coat. He peeled off a one-hundred-dollar bill from the top and handed it to the clerk with a grubby hand.

The boy shoved the change into his backpack without counting it. He sealed the pack with a speed and economy of motion that was impressive. Hefting the pack, he looked up and met Lucan's gaze. Wary eyes filled with panic. He dashed for the door.

Lucan swore under his breath and began to move. Being a plainclothes police detective, he wasn't wearing a uniform. He shouldn't have spooked the kid. And now he was impeded by the people and shelves still between them. The boy took full advantage. By the time Lucan reached the main door, the boy was disappearing around the back of the building.

Lucan sprinted after him. "Hey, wait up a minute!"

The boy never paused. He was through a narrow hole in the crumbling stockade fence behind the building in seconds. Lucan eyed the fence and hesitated. The missing boards were wide enough for the child, but not for him. The remaining fence would never support his weight.

His own house was only a few blocks over, and being a

runner, Lucan knew the neighborhood well. Yet despite his speed and longer legs, there was no sign of the boy when Lucan reached the street behind the store. The row of brand-new townhouses gave way to the original development where Lucan's home was located.

The boy couldn't have gone far. Lucan began searching the area but there was no sign of him. If the boy had gone into one of the houses, there was nothing to tell him which one. A cold wind whipped over his face as he searched the yards. He was certain the boy had ducked in somewhere nearby. Only when a middle-aged woman holding a cell phone stepped out onto her deck demanding to know what he was doing in her yard messing with her Christmas lights did Lucan concede defeat. Flashing his police badge, he apologized for disturbing her and asked about the boy he'd been pursing.

Lips pursed, she told him she didn't know anyone matching that description. She hadn't seen a child like that and she wanted him out of her yard immediately. Lucan returned to the store, where only one other customer remained.

The man paid for his purchase and left. Even so, Salman looked around and lowered his voice when Lucan approached. "He got away?"

"Unfortunately," Lucan admitted ruefully. "He went through the hole in the fence out back."

"I told corporate about that fence. They say it is not their responsibility. The builder put up the fence during construction, so it belongs to the townhouses behind us. Yet the neighbors say it is not their responsibility. What am I to do?" He handed Lucan the hundred-dollar bill the boy had used to pay for his food. "It is real?"

Lucan examined the bill with a frown. "Looks like it to me, but I'm no expert. You said the bank told you the other bills were fine."

Salman nodded. "But a boy like that should not be carrying so much money."

"You got that right. I'll run the serial number just to check, but there's nothing illegal about a boy paying for items with a large bill."

The clerk nodded glumly. "This I know, but there is something wrong."

"Yeah," Lucan agreed, remembering the fear. "How often does he come in?"

"Every day since Sunday. First it was candy and cookies. Then he started buying bread and other items, as you saw. Sunday is my day off, but Ranji tells me that was the day it began."

"And he always pays with a hundred-dollar bill like this one?"

"Yes. That is why I told you about him when you came in today. It is odd. The boy always waits until I am busy, like he did this time. I try to talk to him, but he says nothing. He is very quick."

"I saw how fast he made stuff disappear inside that backpack. Be glad he isn't stealing."

Salman eyed the bill in his hand. "But did he steal this money?"

"Good question. He's definitely afraid of something. Had you seen him in here before he started paying with big bills?"

"No. Never that I can remember. Many neighborhood children come in with and without their parents. One or two have taken something without paying, but most do not. He is not one of the children that I know."

Lucan thought for a moment. "Were any of those town-houses up for sale recently—or unoccupied?"

"This I do not know. Do you not live nearby?"

Lucan rubbed his jaw, feeling tired. "I do, but I've been pulling double shifts lately. When I've had time to go out running I haven't been paying attention. Since you don't recognize him, I'm thinking the kid may be new to the area."

Salman shrugged and Lucan tapped the counter absently. How had a boy of that age come by even one bill of that denomination, let alone those he'd already spent, unless he'd stolen them? This was Wednesday. The kid had been flashing that wad of hundred dollar bills for four days.

He opened his wallet and pulled out a business card. Writing his cell phone number on the back, he handed it to the clerk. "My office number and my cell phone number. Call me if you see him again."

Salman scowled. "You will arrest him?"

"No. He hasn't done anything illegal that we know about. I just want to talk to him and to his parents. There may be a reason he's carrying that kind of cash, but it's dangerous."

"You do not think he stole the money?" Salman repeated the question, frowning intently.

Lucan shrugged. "I don't know, Salman. I'd be more inclined to think that was the case if he was buying junk food and toys, but he picked up peanut butter and bread and even milk. That sounds like hunger to me. His clothing is dirty, and so is he."

And what were the odds the kid had been abandoned?

"He wore the same pants yesterday," Salman confirmed. "Perhaps even the day before, I do not recall for certain."

Lucan knew his frown matched the clerk's. "I'm glad you told me about him when I came in. Like you, I think something is wrong at home. I just want to be sure the kid is safe. If something *is* wrong, we'll intervene for his sake."

Salman shook his head, looking even more worried. "I do not want to cause any trouble."

"Neither do I, Salman. Neither do I. Call me if you see him again."

"Yes, that I will do," the clerk promised unhappily as he pocketed Lucan's card.

Lucan's gaze swept the area as he walked back to his car. He didn't really expect to see the boy again, but he needed to start paying attention to his surroundings. Being tired was no excuse for getting sloppy. The last time he'd been sloppy he'd taken two slugs to the chest and spent months recovering.

Lucan pinched the bridge of his nose before putting the car in gear. A recent spate of robberies had culminated in the murder of a local socialite. The press and politicians were screaming. The entire department was on overtime, and they didn't have a single clue to the thieves' identities. He'd had to cancel his date with Jennifer for the fifth night running. Now she wasn't taking his calls.

Probably he should be more upset. Jennifer was a lot of fun. On the other hand, if she didn't understand what it meant to date a cop, then it was time for him to find a new companion. There was always that nurse who worked with his sister-in-law, Sally. What was her name? Nancy? Nina? Something along those lines. The woman was attractive, and she'd put out plenty of signals that she was interested. The only drawback was that she was a friend of Sally's.

Lucan made it a policy to stay away from friends of family members. They tended to expect their relationships to lead to something permanent. He'd been there and done that and had the divorce papers to prove it. Happily-ever-after only happened in fairy tales. He was no longer interested in anyone with commitment in their eyes.

Abruptly, Lucan realized he was pulling up in front of his house. He hadn't noticed a single thing on the drive home. He swore softly and blinked. There was no missing the fancy sports car with the vanity plate parked in his driveway. Nor could he miss the heavily pregnant woman shutting his front door and locking it before hurrying back toward the driveway. In the twinkling Christmas lights from the houses on either side of his, he could clearly see her stomach bulging beneath the coat she wore unbuttoned. She looked up and paused when she saw his car.

Lucan parked at the curb and got out to greet his sister-in-law. "Hey, Whitney, what's the rush?"

She shook her head and smiled a greeting. "What are you doing home at this hour?"

"It's six forty-four. My shift was over at three."

"Since when do you punch a time clock?"

"I don't. That's why it's six forty-four. Dropping off another care package from Mom, I hope?"

She nodded. "Lasagna, garlic bread and a tossed salad with brownies for desert."

His mouth watered. His Irish mother was an accomplished cook and he knew she was convinced that her only still-single son was going starve to death, since he didn't have a woman of his own to feed him. As a result, she sent frequent meals his way.

"I stopped by to see her on my way home from work," Whitney continued. "She was going to bring it over herself, but she said she was running late so I offered to do it for her since I had to come this way anyhow. I hope you don't mind."

"Are you kidding? Home-cooked food? I'm thrilled."

Whitney smiled back at him. "I put the lasagna and the salad in the refrigerator since I didn't know when you'd get here, but the lasagna is still warm. Everything else is on the counter," Whitney continued. "If I hadn't offered to come over here for her, maybe the two of you could have had dinner together."

He winced. "Thanks for the subtle hint. I meant to go by and see her earlier this week, but I've been so busy...."

"Don't be daft. O'Shays don't do subtle. I know. I married one."

"And we're all glad of it, but you'd better watch out, Mom's brogue is rubbing off on you."

Whitney grinned impishly. "Your mother made enough to feed an army—or you and your three brothers."

Lucan chuckled. "They aren't invited, but you're welcome to join me. Flynn's working today isn't he?" As a fireman, his youngest brother's shift would keep him at the station overnight.

"He is, but I can't stay. I promised my dad and Ruby I'd come by their place for a late supper." She tossed her brownish-blond hair back over her shoulders. "Your mom's worried about you, you know. She says you're working too hard."

"Tell it to the press. They think we're sitting on our hands with this murder. Money talks, you know, and it doesn't hurt that the woman's husband knows everyone on the county council."

He heard the bitterness in his voice and stopped before he really vented about the pressure the force was under to find the thieves-turned-killers working the area. "Besides, you know how my mother likes to worry. I'm surprised she isn't mother-henning you to death about the baby."

"Your mother's great, as you well know, and the baby is on schedule. I've got a week yet and Flynn and I are as ready as we're going to be." She patted her rounded stomach. "Hear that, baby? You can come out now."

"Uh, let's not make it *right* now, okay?"

Whitney laughed and quickly sobered. "You look tired, Lucan."

"I am tired. It goes with the job. You, on the other hand, look gorgeous."

"I look like a pregnant walrus, but thanks just the same."

"Pregnancy becomes you." He nodded toward the car. "I thought you were selling that and buying a sedan."

"We tried selling it, but the deal fell through. If you want it I'll give you a good price."

"Don't tempt me." He'd driven the brightly colored sports car once and been totally hooked. "That's one sweet car."

"But it isn't practical, especially at this time of year."

No, an expensive sports car certainly wasn't practical, but he could dream. Whitney came from money. His family didn't. Even though he knew Whitney would give him the car if she didn't think it would ruffle his pride, a police detective in a flashy sports car like hers just shouted "cop on the take" to his mind.

"We're picking up the new sedan tomorrow," Whitney informed him. "At least think about it. I'll give you a family discount." She smiled easily. "I really hate to go through the whole selling process all over again, but Flynn says it's a thief magnet."

"Flynn's right." And that was another point. The car wouldn't last three minutes in some of the areas he had to work. Still, Lucan gazed at the car wistfully.

"Like I said, think about it, Lucan. I hate to run, but I promised Dad—"

He gave her a brief hug. "Go. I'm amazed you and the kid can still fit behind the steering wheel. And thanks for dropping off dinner. I'll call Mom as soon as I go inside. Maybe I'll take the brownies over and have desert with her. She probably has ice cream to go with them."

"You're as incorrigible as your brother."

Lucan returned her smile. "We're related."

"So true. Good night, Lucan."

"Drive carefully."

He watched Whitney pull out onto the street before returning to his car to move it into the driveway.

The smell of his mother's lasagna hit him the minute he stepped inside. He called her while the oven heated. She had friends coming over for a meeting, so the conversation was short. Whitney would be relieved to learn she couldn't have done dinner with him anyhow. Unfortunately, it also meant he'd have to have his brownies without ice cream unless he wanted to go back to the convenience store.

That thought reminded him of the boy, and he frowned. There was nothing more he could do about that situation tonight. The kid wasn't likely to return to the store any time soon.

BUT LUCAN WAS STILL thinking about the boy in the morning as he ran through the neighborhood. The tree-lined streets were sleepy and peaceful as usual. Nothing struck a chord of concern. There were no houses up for sale and judging by the holiday decorations dotting the houses and yards, the homes were all occupied. The weather had been unexpectedly mild after the cold front that had ushered in the month of December, but according to the weather reports, that was going to change again soon.

Another robbery had been reported last night. The home owners had returned from vacation to find the alarms cut and the house ransacked. Naturally, the owner had to be a close friend of the most outspoken council member—as if the police department didn't have enough pressure to find the thieves. The cases were stacking up.

Lucan spent another fruitless day talking to people and reviewing evidence only to come up empty once more. Frustrated and tired, he finally headed home after seven for a beer and leftover lasagna. He was nearly to the intersection where the convenience store was located when he remembered the boy. Changing direction, he turned down the street behind the convenience store and beyond where the single homes started. Astounded, he spotted the kid, still wearing the same dark coat and grungy pants and toting the green backpack as he hurried down the sidewalk.

Lucan pulled his car to the side of the road and set off after the kid on foot. The boy must have heard the car door because he cast a look over his shoulder and took off running. This time Lucan had the advantage. He got hold of the backpack and spun the boy around until he could grip the boy's arm.

The kid turned into a wild thing, struggling for all he was worth, kicking, punching and wriggling but never making a sound. Lucan had all he could do to hold on to the boy. He tried to calm him down, but the boy was having none of it.

"I'm not going to hurt you. I'm a police officer. Take it easy! You're going to hurt yourself!"

A woman's furious contralto split the air. "Get your hands off him! Help! Police!"

Chapter Two

Lucan jerked his head over his shoulder. He'd been so focused on the boy he hadn't heard the car that was now stopped in the middle of the road. But he certainly heard what proved to be a striking brunette. Knee-high brown leather boots with sexy high heels didn't slow her down a bit. Nor did the pencil slim skirt above them as she ran toward him. Her pretty, delicate features were pinched with fury.

"Lady, I *am* the police!"

She didn't appear to hear him.

"That's my nephew! Let him go, you pervert!"

She swung a matching brown leather shoulder bag at him that looked almost too large for her frame. He turned away, letting his back and side take the brunt of the blow.

"Ow! Stop! What have you got in there? I said stop! I'm a cop!"

Automatically, his left hand came up to block the next swing of the purse, so she kicked him. That fast, the boy eeled away from his grip and took off at a dead run. The kid sprinted across the lawn and disappeared between the houses. Lucan swore. She hit him again.

"Hit or kick me one more time and I'll arrest you for assault." He pulled out his badge case, flipped it open one-handed and thrust it in her face.

She stopped swinging. Taking the leather folder with a perfectly manicured hand, she studied it intently, still radiating fury. Her sassy cap of short brown hair glinted under the streetlamp overhead. The fitted brown leather vest over a soft white blouse hugged nicely rounded breasts. A wide belt cinched at her waist emphasized the trim fit of her skirt. Her jewelry was understated, but the heavy gold bangles circling her wrists weren't costume, and he'd bet neither were the flashing earrings or the simple gold chains at her throat.

Large brown eyes raised from the badge to pierce him in angry disbelief. "Are you really a cop?"

Exasperated, he set his jaw. "Hit me again and you'll see my handcuffs."

She thrust the folder back at him. "What were you doing with my nephew?"

"Trying to ask him some questions."

"That's not how it looked to me." The sexy high-heeled boots brought her nearly to eye level with him at six feet tall. Her glare said she wasn't the least bit intimidated by his badge or his height. "You looked like a pervert trying to kidnap him."

Lucan tried counting to ten. He didn't make it past four. That heart-shaped face and creamy smooth skin might tempt a man to want to learn more about her, but the shrew's temper would quickly squash the idea. "Let me see your driver's license."

Her eyes snapped fire. Lucan held that gaze, narrowing his own eyes and waiting. Scowling, she opened her purse. A thirty-eight revolver was clearly visible despite the jumble of items inside.

Lucan jerked the purse from her grasp. Letting it fall to the ground, he spun her around. "You're under arrest."

"What?"

He snapped handcuffs into place.

"Let me go! You can't arrest me for calling you a pervert."

His jaw clenched. "No, but I can arrest you for carrying a concealed weapon, impeding an officer in the performance of his duty and assault on a police officer." He glanced at the expensive car with its engine still running, sitting in the middle of the street, and steered her up against it. "And impeding the flow of traffic," he added.

"You have to be kidding!"

She struggled as he patted her down quickly and impersonally despite the fact that the body beneath his hands was made for a different sort of patting entirely.

"You have the right to remain silent—"

"Oh, for crying out loud. I know my rights. I'm a lawyer."

He managed to silence the oath that sprang to his lips and continued reciting the Miranda rights.

"What about Kip?" she demanded. "Don't you understand? Something is wrong!"

The rising tenor of her tone almost stopped him, but he finished and held the stormy gaze she tossed over her shoulder at him. "Do you understand these rights as stated?"

"Yes!"

He stepped back and let her turn around. She tossed aside a drift of hair that had fallen across one eye and glared furiously.

"I apologize," she offered without a trace of apology in her tone or manner. "But you were manhandling my nephew. It made me see red."

"I was not manhandling him!" He lowered his voice wondering why he was letting this woman get to him. "Your nephew was kicking me."

"Because you grabbed him. I saw you."

Lucan swallowed a retort. "Lady, I'm not going to stand out here and argue with you."

The scene probably *had* looked bad from a concerned

relative's point of view, but he was not about to concede that point. "If you're the kid's aunt, how come he took off?"

A flash of chagrin. She swung her head as if trying to toss long hair over her shoulder only to realize it wasn't there.

"I live in Boston. I haven't seen Kip in a couple of years." Her eyes narrowed once more. "And you were scaring him to death."

The boy *had* been scared.

Her striking blue eyes clouded. "I'm sorry I overreacted. It's been a long day and there was no way I could know you were a cop when I intervened."

She still didn't sound contrite.

"We're on the same side, Officer," she added defiantly.

"Detective."

She gave a negligent shrug.

Lucan reached for her handbag. This woman knew how to press his buttons. Under her watchful gaze he removed the revolver. "You want to explain this?"

Her frown twisted to annoyance. "I forgot it was in there."

Lucan waited. Even her sigh was angry. "It's completely legal. I have permits to carry concealed, *Detective*. You'll find them in my purse."

Lucan gritted his teeth, determined not to let her climb under his skin. The purse was so jammed with stuff he was surprised she could get it closed. No wonder it had felt like bricks when she hit him. The weapon was fully loaded. Beneath it sat a canister of pepper spray.

"Expecting a war?"

"I like to be prepared."

He held his temper along with her gaze. "You aren't a cop."

"No, I told you, I'm a lawyer."

"Then you don't have a permit to carry concealed in Maryland."

Irritation flashed in those bright blue eyes. "I'm an officer of the court, detective. I assure you all my paperwork is in order."

"Uh-huh. Well as an officer of the court, you should know the state of Maryland doesn't recognize the right to carry concealed weapons for anyone outside of law enforcement."

If looks could burn, he'd be sizzling. It was her turn to grit perfectly even white teeth.

"It was an oversight. When I left work I forgot the gun was in there or I would have taken it out."

He pulled out the pepper spray. "Boston must be rougher than I thought. Am I going to find a switchblade next?"

"No!"

"Good." Lucan dug until he found the paperwork. A passport was there as well. That started a whole new set of alarm bells clanging.

"Planning a trip out of the country?"

"Yes. If you must know, my sister and I are taking her children on vacation this weekend. We're flying to Bermuda."

"Uh-huh. In December. Right before Christmas."

"Can you think of a better time?"

Lucan eyed her. "Does your sister have a husband?" Her gaze flickered. He pressed home his point. "Does *he* know about your vacation plans?"

Her gaze dropped for an instant before challenging him once more. "That's none of your business."

"It is if he has custody and no knowledge of your plans."

There was relief in her posture. "He doesn't have custody. Milt's her *second* husband. The children are all hers."

Bingo. This was a family dispute of some sort. Reason enough for the kid to run off. If it wasn't for all the money the boy was flashing around, Lucan might be tempted to dismiss the situation. As it was, however… "Are your plane tickets in here as well?"

"No. We haven't booked our flight yet." She flushed. "Okay, I know this sounds odd."

He kept his expression neutral. Suddenly the fight seemed to go out of her.

"Look, something is wrong at my sister's place. She was supposed to call me on Sunday to firm up our plans. She never called."

Concern clouded her features. Lucan tried to determine if it was real. He had the impression of genuine emotion, but how could he tell?

"I haven't been able to reach Casey all week. I wanted to come sooner but I had to finish a case before I could leave. You have my gun permits."

"Permits, plural?"

"Yes."

From inside her purse he pulled out an envelope he'd shifted while looking for her wallet. Kyra Wolfstead was licensed to carry a concealed weapon in the state of Massachusetts and two neighboring states.

He opened her bulging leather wallet and studied her driver's license. The names matched. Her photo was crisp and clear. Lucan had a feeling cameras of any sort liked Kyra Wolfstead. He could understand their approval. If they'd met under different circumstances, he might approve as well.

"I have business cards in there too," she added.

And a thick wad of cash that brought his head up sharply.

"I didn't want to waste time going to an ATM after I got here," she explained before he could ask.

Her tone was calm and brisk, but annoyance flashed once more. "We're wasting time, Off—Detective. Casey has an ex-husband with a court injunction against him."

Which could easily be checked out and just might

explain the arsenal and the passport. Lucan lifted one of the business cards and scowled. "This says you're an insurance investigator."

She sighed. "I work for Dowlings Limited, as you can see. They are similar to Lloyds of London."

"I've heard of Dowlings. So are you an investigator or a lawyer?"

"I'm both. I worked in international law for a time, which comes in handy with my current job. Many of our clients have places outside of the United States. Art objects and jewelry are often fenced in other countries. I know the laws and restrictions in many of those jurisdictions. Look, could we have this discussion later? I have an unusual job and it's nice that you're interested, but I'd like to go to my sister's place and make sure Casey is okay. I'm deeply concerned."

Headlights speared them as an approaching car slowed. In the time they'd been talking, dusk had settled over the neighborhood. The driver of the oncoming car swung into the opposite lane on the narrow street to pass Kyra's car, which was still sitting there with its engine running. A woman and two children stared curiously at them as they drove by. Lucan's car was parked half a block away, and he'd left his radio inside.

"Have a seat on the lawn under that tree." He indicated an old elm with a wave of his hand. Kyra Wolfstead glared daggers. He raised a hand to forestall her next protest. "I need to move your car out of the middle of the street."

"For pity's sake. The ground is freezing."

"I'll hurry."

"You'd better." She strode to the tree without waiting for assistance and folded gracefully onto the yellowed grass. Lucan thought she might be trembling the slightest bit, but he read that as anger rather than fear.

Unloading her gun, he tucked the weapon in the back of his waistband, pocketing the shells. He removed the pepper spray and put that in his pocket as well. Then he drove her car to the side of the road.

In the back seat was a rich-looking, long leather coat that would no doubt match the boots and gloves. There was also an overnight-sized suitcase, a brown soft leather briefcase, what appeared to be a computer bag and two plastic sacks of brightly wrapped packages. An expensive GPS system sat on the dashboard displaying the car's location. A set of printed directions from the Internet lay on the passenger's seat beside a thermos.

Lucan opened the thermos and sniffed the contents. Some sort of spiced tea if he wasn't mistaken, still warm. A sealed plastic drinking bottle was half full of what appeared to be water. This was a woman who obviously liked backup plans.

He checked the destination on the GPS device against the printed directions. They matched. The address was one block over. In the glove compartment, her registration was in order. The address matched the one on her driver's license and the gun permits.

It appeared she was telling the truth. Still, that wad of cash and the weapon were a cause for concern. While this might be nothing more than a domestic dispute, there was a little boy running around with his own wad of cash.

Locking the car, Lucan went to where she sat and reached down to help her to her feet. She stiffened at his touch, but flowed up easily despite the skirt and heels.

"My car's down the street," he told her.

"Are you going to undo the cuffs?"

"No."

"You're really going to arrest me?" Despite her high-heeled boots, she kept pace with him easily. She had an athlete's body. Lean and trim. He wondered if she was a runner.

"That remains to be seen," he answered frankly.

He had her sit on the back seat of his car with her legs

out while he ran her information. She seethed with impatience, but clamped her lips tightly against the complaint he could read so easily in her expressive features.

Unsurprised when she checked out clean, Lucan still hesitated before pulling her out of the car and releasing the cuffs. He handed her back her purse.

"I'll follow you to your sister's place."

"You aren't going to arrest me?" She all but vibrated with anger.

"I've had my quota of paperwork for the day, but push me and I'll make an exception."

She extended her hand. "And my gun?"

"Is illegal in Maryland." He didn't add that he didn't like civilians with guns. "By all rights I should be taking you in for possession."

"But you won't?"

Lucan shook his head. "The jury's still out on that, counselor. Let's go see what your sister has to say."

She pursed her lips. Turning on her sexy high heels she returned to her car, anger in every stride. He watched the tight sway of her body in that nicely fitted skirt, and his lips curved. Angry or not, Kyra Wolfstead was a very sexy, intriguing package. Too bad they hadn't met socially.

She drove to the next block and pulled into the driveway of a small stone-and-vinyl-sided two-story house. An ancient Chinese elm covered most of the front yard. A tattered swing and several beat-up lawn chairs graced a wide front porch. A child's bike with a flat rear tire leaned drunkenly against the side of the house.

There was nothing out of the ordinary in the setting. Lucan had passed this house several times on his morning runs. Only now did he notice that the drapes were pulled tight. And while the majority of the neighbors' houses sported brightly colored Christmas lights and door decorations, this house was dark and forlorn-looking by comparison.

Kyra pulled into the driveway. She didn't wait, but hurried to the front porch. Her large purse flopped against her side. He caught up with her as she pressed the doorbell. When there was no response, she rapped loudly and tried the doorknob.

"Locked." She looked affronted.

"Your sister may be out."

"No. Something's wrong. I tried calling her cell phone again from the car. She always carries her cell phone and keeps it on because of the children, but my calls are going straight to voice mail."

"Maybe her battery went dead," he suggested as she began trying windows. "Lots of people forget to charge their cell phones. What are you doing? As a lawyer, you know you can't break into her house."

"It's illegal entry if I don't break anything to get in," she corrected.

His lips curved. It was hard not to like her even if she was a pain in the neck. He followed her to the locked side door and on to the back porch with the same results.

"Does your sister work?"

"She's a waitress." Kyra changed directions, heading for the single car detached garage. The side door opened easily beneath her fingers.

Lucan yanked her back when she would have gone inside. He was starting to have a bad feeling about this situation.

"Wait."

"Her car's in there!"

"I said, wait!"

Unhappily, she did, tapping her foot in annoyance. The seven-year-old sedan inside was locked and empty save for two children's car seats. Eyeing the trunk, he turned to Kyra only to find her going rapidly back toward the rear of the house.

Lucan started after her. "I'm going to call—what are you doing? Don't—"

She lifted a child's lawn chair from a pile of matted leaves, strode onto the porch and up to the kitchen window. Before he could reach her, she'd swung the chair at the pane with surprising force. The glass shattered into a million pieces.

"Now it's breaking and entering," she told him without looking his way. "You can arrest me later."

Using the chair to clear away the broken shards, she poked her head inside. Her gasp had him reaching for her as she recoiled.

Chapter Three

The putrid stench that filled her nostrils made Kyra gag. She jerked her head back, barely aware of the hands pulling her away from the window. Tears swam in her eyes as she sucked air greedily into her lungs. Her worst nightmare had just been confirmed. Casey had to be dead.

Kyra barely heard the detective calling in the scene. She kept seeing the kitchen with dishes, food, flour and sugar canisters tossed about the room. Decaying meat and once-frozen foods rotted on the floor. And most chilling of all were the small footprints leading in and out of the mess.

She swayed. Hands pressed her down onto the back porch steps. He forced her head down to her knees.

"Breathe. Slow, deep breaths."

"She's dead."

"We don't know that yet. Sit still. I don't need you passing out on me."

That jerked her head up. "I'm not going to pass out."

"Could have fooled me. Sit."

"My sister—"

"If she's in there, we'll find her. That damage wasn't done today. I have officers en route."

"Kip!"

His tone gentled, but there was no mistaking the iron will behind his words. "We'll find the boy. I promise."

She shook her head, fighting tears. "No wonder he ran from us."

"We'll find him," he repeated firmly.

"And the others?"

His expression blanked, then hardened. "How many others?"

"Two. Brian and Maggie. Brian's five. Maggie just turned three."

And the horror of those small footprints hit her again. Her stomach lurched. She swallowed hard, determined to conquer the upheaval in her stomach. If only she'd come sooner. She should have turned her case over to one of her colleagues. Hadn't she known Monday night that something was wrong? If Casey was dead...

"Ms. Wolfshead. Kyra! Listen to me. I'm going to go around to the front of the house. I want you to come with me."

It took her first name in that deep voice to get her attention. Eyes that had been chips of granite earlier were a warm, sympathetic gray now. She would not cry.

"I'm okay."

"I know you are. Come on."

In no time vehicles and people began arriving. Despite her need to see for herself what had happened inside, she obeyed the detective's order and sat shivering on the porch swing under the watchful eye of a uniformed officer.

Long minutes dragged by before her detective returned. His features were grim. Her stomach dropped.

"No." He shook his head moving quickly to her side.

She was on her feet, swaying, with no memory of having moved.

"The house is empty. There's no one inside," he assured her.

"But where—?"

"We're canvassing the neighborhood. We know your

nephew is somewhere nearby. Hopefully he can tell us what happened and where your sister and the other children are. Maybe they're staying with a neighbor."

Kyra shook her head. "They don't know any neighbors. They just moved in a couple of weeks ago. I need to go inside. I need to see—"

"Give us a few minutes to process the scene. We need photos and prints before I can let anyone in there."

She knew that. Anyone who watched crime shows on television knew that.

"Is the whole house like the kitchen?"

"Yes. This will take time. Are you going to be all right?"

Not if Casey was dead. *Please don't let her be dead.* She shivered hard.

"I'm fine."

He recognized the lie, but nodded all the same. Removing his jacket he handed it to her. "Put this on."

"I don't—"

"For once, will you stop arguing and do what I say?"

"You'll get cold."

His smile was so gentle, her heart constricted.

"The house has heat, Kyra. I'll be fine. Wait here." He patted her shoulder before turning away.

The coat had a light, clean, masculine scent and she inhaled deeply, burrowing into its warmth even though nothing would make her warm again. Casey was dead. She had to be dead. And the children. Where were the children?

Kyra had no idea how long she waited before he came back outside and joined her on the swing. He rested his hand on her arm and she felt that touch despite the cloth between them.

"We're waiting for the local electric company to arrive. They need to restore power to the house."

"Why isn't there any power?"

He grimaced. "The line was cut. Tell me about your

sister, Kyra," he continued before she could say anything else. "You said she has an ex-husband."

"Milt Bowman. He's an engineer with Norris Transportation Systems, a local contracting firm. Casey has a restraining order against him."

"He's hit her? Been abusive?"

Kyra nodded, swallowing fear-laced bile. "Only when he's drunk. He gets mean when he drinks. Casey covered for him for years, but one night he went after Kip. She stopped him and he broke her jaw. As soon as he passed out, she took the kids to a shelter. They got her to the hospital, helped her get a lawyer and a restraining order, and she filed for divorce. When Milt realized she wasn't going to change her mind, he backed off and agreed to the divorce. In exchange she refused to file charges."

That still angered her, but there was no arguing once Casey made up her mind.

"Then she met Jordan Fillmont. They started dating."

Kyra tried not to let her feelings about that show.

"They married the day her divorce became final."

And no amount of talk could convince her sister not to rush into another marriage. Casey didn't like being a single parent.

"Milt was furious," Kyra continued. "He threatened her."

"She went to the police?"

"Yes. She applied for another restraining order. Milt hired a lawyer to sue for joint custody."

"He wants the kids?"

"Of course not. He wants to make her pay for getting remarried. He's a drunk and a jerk. My sister has terrible taste in men."

She didn't add that it seemed to be a family trait.

"Including her new husband?"

Kyra bit the tip of her tongue before answering. "I don't know him. They were married a few months ago."

"Where does Fillmont work?"

"The Oak Forest Country Club. I'm not sure what he does there, something to do with the golf course, I think."

"O'Shay?" someone called.

"Be right there." He turned back to her. "Sit here a little longer, all right?"

His hand was warm on hers. She wondered when he'd taken it. Now he gave her fingers a gentle squeeze and stood, leaving her to talk with a pair of plain clothes officers. After a moment the three disappeared inside the house.

The power company arrived and the repair crew was ushered through the police line. Time trickled past. Her watch was at a jeweler's being repaired, so she had no idea how late it was. She fidgeted, needing to be doing something besides sitting and thinking in circles. Anxious now, she waited for the detective to return. When he did, he motioned for her to join him.

"This is Detective Todd Berringer and Captain Walsh, Kyra."

She barely acknowledged the introduction. Her eyes riveted on what she could see of the living-room disaster through the open front door. She stepped past them and moved inside, surveying the scene in sick dread. Every stick of furniture had been sliced open. Every breakable object had been broken in sheer, wanton destruction. An undecorated artificial Christmas tree lay on its side, a box of ornaments crushed beneath it.

Tears blurred her vision. She blinked hard to hold them at bay. "Why?"

"It appears someone was looking for something," one of the men said.

Kyra shook her head, keeping her eyes averted until she felt more in control. "My sister doesn't have anything of value. Maybe a few pieces of jewelry, but this…"

Helplessly she stared at a handmade ornament that had rolled nearly to the door. She lifted it gently. Kip had made this when he was in kindergarten. She had a blue one just like it.

"Ms. Wolfstead, I'm sorry, but is this your sister?" Detective Berringer removed a picture from a shattered glass frame and handed her the torn photograph.

Casey and the children smiled up at her. The photo had been taken more than a year ago. Kyra carried a wallet-sized version in her purse.

The tears came close to spilling over as she stared at the photo. Everyone always commented on how much Kyra resembled her older sister. It was several seconds before she could do more than nod. "Yes. And that's Kip, Brian and Maggie."

He produced another photo in a cracked plastic frame that showed Casey and Jordan standing outside the courthouse on their wedding day. She had a copy of that picture as well.

"That's Casey and her husband, Jordan," she confirmed. "Is the entire house like this?"

"Pretty much."

"Did you find…?" She couldn't bring herself to say *blood,* but Detective O'Shay was there, touching her lightly.

"There's no blood, Kyra. Nothing to tell us if this mess happened while the family was still here or if they came home to find the house like this. We know Kip is alive. There's no reason to think the rest of the family isn't as well."

More than anything she wanted to believe him, but seeing this destruction… "Casey would have called me if she could have."

The men exchanged looks. It was Detective Berringer who spoke again. "Ms. Wolfstead, you say your sister didn't have anything of value. What about cash? Some people don't like banks."

"My sister's a waitress. Her husband works at a country club. They don't have a lot of cash."

Once again Detective O'Shay touched her arm lightly.

There was an almost apologetic expression in those deep gray eyes.

"Kip has been going into the local convenience store since Monday. He's been buying food and carrying it away in his backpack. Every purchase has been paid for with a one-hundred-dollar bill."

For a second she didn't understand what he was telling her. Then she couldn't breathe. "That's crazy." The words came out as a whisper.

"Could your sister or her husband be involved in drugs, Ms. Wolfstead?" Detective Berringer asked.

"What? No! Casey has children!"

The men exchanged another look. She could almost hear the silent question that passed between them. How well did she really know her sister? Choking back a protest, she forced herself to think. Even unvoiced, it was a valid question and it deserved an honest answer.

"I was a senior in high school when Casey married Milt. There are eleven years between us." And the difference in their ages had kept them from being as close as she would have liked. "But she's my sister. We keep in touch, even though we don't see each other very often. My job's in Boston. Casey lives here."

Was it possible? Could Casey be using drugs? Would Kyra know if she was? Yes, she was sure she'd know. Casey was her sister!

"My sister isn't into drugs," she stated more firmly. "I can't speak for her husband, but look at this house. They rent. They don't even own this place. She's had that same shabby Christmas tree since before Kip was born. If they had the sort of money drug-dealing is supposed to net, don't you think they'd live better than this? My sister drives a seven-year-old car! It's always breaking down. I've sent her money for repairs. Jordan's no bigwig. I won't believe they're involved in drugs."

Detective O'Shay's gaze bored into hers. "Drug habits are expensive."

Kyra closed her eyes. "I don't believe it. I don't want to believe it," she added more softly.

"I understand, but where would Kip get several hundred dollars in cash?"

"I don't know!" Her voice fell to almost a whisper. "I don't know."

And she still wanted to cry, but now her eyes felt dry and scratchy. In order to help Casey and the children, she needed to remain calm and answer their questions. And they had a lot of questions. It was dismaying to realize how few answers she could give. Tired beyond thought, she finally shook her head. "May I look around? Maybe I'll see something that will help."

Detective O'Shay nodded. "I was going to ask you to do that."

She drew strength from his solid presence as they moved silently from room to room. The downstairs and the master bedroom had been the focus of the destruction. The children's rooms showed more cursory searches. In those rooms, drawers and closets had been rifled and the mattresses had been sliced open and overturned, but the damage wasn't nearly as bad as in the other rooms. Maggie's bedroom had barely been disturbed at all.

Decorated in pastels, her tiny room had obviously been intended as an office. A built-in bookcase sat along one wall where a closet should have been. Stuffed toys and children's books had been pulled from the shelves. The dresser drawers had been dumped but nothing was broken.

"Where are the pillows and blankets?" she asked as they stood in the hall after going through each room. The detective looked puzzled. She indicated one of the boys' rooms. "There are no blankets or pillows in any of the children's rooms."

His lips parted. He returned to the master bedroom at the far end of the hall and flicked on the light.

"There are blankets and pillows in here. They're ripped, but they're here."

He crossed to the room she'd indicated and studied the scene.

"Good observation, Kyra. We should have noticed that."

He pinched the bridge of his nose as if he had a headache. She'd tried hard not to notice how attractive he was despite the lines that bracketed his mouth and eyes. Sure, he needed a shave. And what appeared to be a recent haircut couldn't tame his dark, unruly hair. But he carried himself with an aura of command that was very appealing. His mannerisms said he was sure of his place in the universe. His expression was stern, but those tired gray eyes held empathy and genuine concern.

"Someone could have used the blankets to wrap the children in to carry them away."

He was thinking out loud, but she shook her head.

"Kip's still nearby, and why take the pillows?" She thought for a moment. "It's getting cold out there, but it's been fairly warm in Boston until now. Is there a tree house in the neighborhood?"

"I'm glad one of us is still thinking. Todd!"

The other detective bounded up the stairs. The search for a tree house or a shed was put in motion.

Kyra was in the living room moving cushions aside when Detective O'Shay returned to her.

"What are you doing?"

"Looking for her purse."

"We didn't find one." He held up his hand before she could speak again. "We looked."

"Doesn't that strike you as odd? If someone took her, wouldn't you expect her purse to still be here?" She gave him a flat stare. "I don't see someone saying 'get your purse, we're kidnapping you.'"

"We don't know she was kidnapped, Kyra."

"No. We don't."

"Ms. Wolfstead—"

"Stick with Kyra, Detective. It's late and I'm too tired for formality."

The lines around his mouth deepened, but she couldn't tell if it was from amusement or annoyance.

"It is late. Where are you planning to stay tonight?"

"Right here."

This time there was no question. He was annoyed. "That's out of the question."

"Why?"

"This is a crime scene."

"One you've already processed," she reminded him.

His hand swept the room indicating the mess. "You can't stay here."

"Can and am." She set her jaw, taking what her colleagues called her fighting stance. "If Casey or the children are nearby, this is where they'll come. I'm not leaving."

His eyes narrowed. He didn't glance at his partner when the other man strolled over to them. His focus was entirely on her.

"I can make that an order."

Kyra raised her chin. "That would be petty. You've searched this place from top to bottom. I'm staying."

"There's nowhere for you to sleep."

She reached up to toss back her long hair, remembered she'd had it cut and restyled on Saturday and brushed some hair back from her face instead. "Your concern is touching. Do you really think I'm going to sleep tonight, Detective?"

"We kicked in the front door," he pointed out. "And the back window is broken."

"You can board up the window and I can prop the front door closed with a chair if the lock is broken."

His thunderous expression told her what he thought of that.

"Be reasonable, Detective. Someone's already torn the

place apart. Do you really think they're going to come back tonight?"

"That isn't the point."

She narrowed her eyes. "Then what is the point? This is my sister's home. I'm not leaving."

He muttered something under his breath. His partner looked away, lips curving.

"Ms. Wolfstead, I don't have the manpower to station someone here to protect you."

"Protect me from what? If they didn't get what they came for, they know it isn't here. If they did get it, they aren't coming back. I'll be perfectly safe."

He muttered something else under his breath. "No, and that's final."

"Very well. I'll spend the night in my car out front."

The other detective snorted. Lucan gave him a look that sent him moving away.

"Look, Detective, you've taken photos, dusted for prints and searched the house. Let me stay and at least see if I can clean some of this mess."

"It's late."

"And getting later," she agreed. "Go home, Detective. Get some sleep. One of us should."

He closed his eyes, opened them again and lowered his voice. "There's still the matter of an illegal weapon."

Kyra's stomach did a quick flip and roll, but she refused to back down. She held his gaze and projected a false calm. "Are you going to charge me?"

"I should."

She read victory in his words and released a breath she hadn't known she was holding.

"You aren't going to be reasonable about this, are you?" he growled.

"I'm always reasonable."

He cocked his head in patent disbelief.

She held up her hand. "I'm also very determined. This is my *family,* Detective. I *have* to be here. While I appreciate your help, go home. There's nothing more you can do here tonight."

His displeasure was obvious. He tried staring her down, but she'd faced too many other dominant males in her chosen career to be intimidated by looks or words. She wasn't leaving until she found her sister.

He swore softly. Everyone else in the room was studiously looking the other way. She had no doubt they were listening intently so she was surprised when, with a quick glance around, the detective withdrew her gun from his waistband and handed it to her.

"I never saw this," he told her gruffly in a voice barely above a whisper. "I don't ever want to see it. Are we clear?"

"Perfectly." She thrust it into her purse, deciding now wasn't the time to demand the bullets as well. Was he really worried about her safety? Detective O'Shay was a hard man to read.

He handed her the canister of pepper spray, then withdrew a business card and scrawled a number across the back before handing her the card.

"My cell phone number. I live one block over. If anything happens or if you find anything or even think of anything I should know, call me. I can be here in minutes."

Kyra took the proffered card, feeling inexplicably soothed. Good-looking and caring was a nice combination in a man. Lucan. His first name was Lucan.

"Come on," he continued. "I'll give you a hand in the kitchen."

Startled, she tried not to gape. "That isn't necessary."

"Yes ma'am, it is. My mother would flay me with dark looks for months if I left you with that mess and went home to bed. I can at least get the rotted food out of here. Todd and I need to put some plywood across the window anyhow. I saw some in the garage. Todd!"

There'd been a trace of a brogue in his voice, she was sure of it. Second-generation Irish?

In no time he and his fellow officers had cleared the worst of the kitchen mess and nailed plywood over the window she had broken. Lucan checked out the front door and pronounced it useable.

"The dead bolt wasn't on when we broke in so it still works," he told her, checking to make sure the door closed and stayed closed. "I'll have patrol cars swing by here as often as possible, but you should know the phones don't work. The line was cut."

Another item that didn't bode well for Casey. Kyra shoved that thought down hard. "That's okay, I have my cell phone."

He nodded. "Do you want anything out of your car?"

"My coat and the suitcase on the back seat, but I can manage."

"I'll get them."

Bemused, she waited alongside Detective Berringer while her small suitcase and leather duster were carried inside. She removed Lucan's suitcoat and handed it over, immediately missing the warmth and the light spicy scent.

"Call if you need anything."

"Thank you. Both of you."

"Just doin' our job, ma'am," Detective Berringer told her. Her detective merely tipped his head. Together they left.

And when had Detective Lucan O'Shay become *her* detective?

They stopped outside and spoke quietly at the curb for several minutes. Kyra watched until they finally got in their separate vehicles and pulled away. She wasn't sure, but she thought Detective O'Shay stared her way before leaving. Then she was alone in the dark, smelly house with only her fear for company.

There wasn't a prayer she was going to sleep tonight despite the exhaustion tugging at her body. Her mind was too busy with fear and recriminations. She should have been hungry, but she wasn't. The thought of food revolted her. And she had a sudden mad impulse to call Simon Testier.

Her coworker and former lover was an excellent investigator and he just might think of something she was missing. She'd been pretty hard on him before he'd left for Germany. But Simon wouldn't take no for an answer. She'd been trying to break up with him for over a month now, and the egotistical jerk couldn't believe she was serious.

Staring at the kitchen clock she computed the time and realized it was only five-thirty in the morning where he was. Simon hated mornings. That made the idea all the more tempting, but she stifled the impulse.

She didn't want to do anything that would encourage Simon to believe she was reconsidering their relationship. Sighing, she salvaged what she could of her sister's tree ornaments. Most of the glass ones were broken, including the handful that had survived their own childhood. Several of the handmade ones were intact, but somehow that almost made it worse.

Smoothing out a paper angel that had been one of her mother's favorites, Kyra allowed a few tears to roll down her cheeks, before hunting up a vacuum cleaner. Cleaning gave her a channel for the pain and fear. As she turned off the vacuum, she froze.

Had she just heard someone whispering?

Goose bumps chased up her arms. She listened hard, but the house was silent except for the noise of the blower as the furnace started up once more. Had it been her imagination working overtime? She was tired. But what if she'd really heard someone?

Impossible. The police had searched the house from top to bottom.

But what if they had missed something?

"Kip?" Her voice sounded loud in the silence. She strained to hear the slightest sound. "Kip, it's Aunt Kyra. Are you here?"

Even the house seemed to hold its breath. Her pulse thundered in her ears.

"It's okay to come out now. I'm here to help."

Nothing. No sound. Calming her racing heart she stared at the staircase for what seemed like a very long time, listening to the noises of the old house. There was no other sound.

It must have been wishful thinking. If she didn't get control of herself she'd be useless when they did find Casey. And they would, she vowed. She wasn't leaving until she found her sister and her children. Maybe Kyra should take a break and try to rest.

The patter of small running footsteps overhead was real and distinct.

Her heart slammed into her throat. She flew up the steps calling Kip's name. No one answered. There was no sound as she reached the dark landing. Surely if the children were here the police would have found them. Still, she went from room to empty room.

No footsteps. No voices. She was alone in the house and losing her mind.

Shaking all over, her gaze was drawn to the front window in the master bedroom. The drapes had been pulled back, giving her a view of the night beyond. A patrol car moved slowly down the street.

Kyra crossed to watch until the car turned the corner and disappeared. One quick phone call and they'd return. They could search the house with her. Did she want that?

The police had looked. She had looked. There was no one in the house. She didn't want them to think she was crazy.

The crisp winter night spread out still and silent below her. She stood a long time with her forehead pressed against the cold glass, silently praying that Casey and the children were somewhere safe in the darkness.

If her sister was found unharmed, Kyra swore she'd make a serious effort to get to know Casey and her kids better. Kyra enjoyed her busy life, but she sacrificed a lot for her job. She was rarely home. Her work required a great deal of travel, and Simon had enjoyed finding remote places to vacation.

She and Casey stayed in contact by phone and e-mail, but it wasn't enough. Casey was the only close family Kyra had. Though her sister was so much older, Kyra should have made more time for her as well.

"Just let Casey be all right," she whispered silently to the darkness outside.

Turning around, her step faltered. Had she just seen a small shadow dart away near the end of the dark hall?

Chapter Four

Before Lucan could knock, the front door flew open. Kyra Wolfstead stood there, five foot seven inches of determination despite the exhaustion rimming the tired blue eyes that gazed at him. Lucan cocked his head.

"I am not crazy," she announced.

He blinked. "Okay."

"Don't placate me."

He held up his palms. "It's three forty-two in the morning. I'm not awake enough to bother."

She swiped at her hair. "I know what I saw."

"A shadow."

"There was someone in the hall upstairs. A child!"

He stepped past her. The living room showed that she must have indeed spent the entire night cleaning. The broken Christmas tree was in its stand in the corner looking sadly forlorn. Garland, bows and ornaments, laid out neatly, covered the battered remains of the couch. The floor had been vacuumed clean of broken glass and stuffing. All the furniture was in upright positions.

"Did you even try to sleep?"

"No. So I couldn't have been dreaming. And I wasn't hallucinating," she told him intently.

He shrugged. "Okay."

"Stop saying that!"

He spread his hands defensively. "Tell me again exactly what you saw, Kyra."

"First I thought I heard whispering, but I wasn't sure. I'd been running the vacuum cleaner and when I turned it off…" She looked toward the stairs. "I called out but no one answered. Then I heard footsteps running across the floor overhead. I ran upstairs but the rooms were all empty. I thought my mind was playing tricks on me."

Lucan heard the desperation in her rising tone. She took a deep breath, firm round breasts rising beneath her sweater as she pushed at her hair absently.

"I watched the patrol car drive past from the master-bedroom window. I guess I stood there for several minutes after they went past." Her gaze defied him to criticize.

"You're tired, Kyra."

"Of course I'm tired! But I didn't imagine that shadow at the end of the hall. I think Kip is in the house. I saw what I saw!"

Lucan heaved a tired sigh. "I'm not saying you didn't." He rubbed at the stubble along his jaw. Her call had pulled him from sleep and he was feeling as rough as his stubble. He'd tugged on the nearest clothes at hand and rushed over.

"I'm not crazy," she repeated.

He closed eyes gritty from lack of sleep and opened them again. "I don't think you're crazy. Let's go have another look around."

"Then you believe me?"

"I'm here, aren't I?" He started up the stairs and paused. "Did you check all the doors and windows?"

"Before I went upstairs."

"But not since you thought you saw someone?"

"You think someone came in after I went upstairs?"

"I just want to get the sequence straight. Finding an open door or window might mean exactly that. Let's take a look."

"I suppose Kip could have a key to the house."

Lucan nodded. "There are a lot of latch-key kids around."

She trailed him as he checked the doors and windows in each room. Everything was locked tight and the plywood over the kitchen window was undisturbed. The kitchen was clean enough to meet his mother's approval.

"You really have been busy."

Wearily, she shrugged. "I did what I could."

She followed him to the stairs. "I keep wondering if Milt did this out of spite. Casey said his temper is terrible when he's drunk. Maybe she came home and found him trashing the house. I keep thinking he killed her, maybe all of them. Maybe Kip is the only one who got away."

Her voice broke. He took her arm, turning her to face him. Tears filled her eyes and she looked down, blinking hard. Her coping mechanisms were starting to fail as lack of sleep battered her tired brain.

"You need to rest, Kyra. There's no evidence to support anyone being killed here."

"Then where is she? Maybe she came in and he strangled her or forced her away at gunpoint."

He tilted her chin up, forcing her to meet his gaze. "Don't do this. You aren't helping Casey or the children by going to pieces."

Anger, hurt and fear swam in her eyes. She closed them and took a shuddery breath. "You're right. I'm sorry. I'm not usually so emotional."

He let go of her and stepped back, watching her draw on her fragile reserves. "I know. Let's go up and have another look around."

Kyra turned and began ascending the stairs.

"Does Casey's ex own a gun?"

She considered before answering and when she did her voice was stronger, less emotional.

"I don't know. I don't think so. I think Casey would have mentioned it if he did, but I barely knew the man."

"What about Casey?"

She stopped near the top of the steps. "What do you mean?"

"Does she own a gun?"

Kyra started to answer and stopped. There was dejection in the sudden slump of her shoulders.

"I don't know."

The words were a whisper. Lucan nodded. "Could she be using drugs?"

Anger flashed in her eyes. "You keep harping on that! I haven't changed my answer. I can't see Casey involved in drugs or condoning their use in any way shape or form. She loves her kids. She would never do that!"

No need to point out she didn't seem to know her sister all that well. "But her new husband might?"

She continued up the stairs without answering. Experience told Lucan a drug connection was most likely the scenario behind this sort of destruction. That didn't make it so, and he was keeping an open mind, but Kyra needed to accept the possibility.

He grimaced. Actually, she was handling everything far better than he would in her place. The woman needed some sleep. They both did.

Her cleaning efforts had stopped downstairs, he noticed after walking through each room once again. Nothing up here had changed. Lucan took the children's step stool from the bathroom and used it to pull down the trap door in the hall ceiling. Narrow steps unfolded leading up to the attic.

"I didn't even notice that."

Kyra's expression was dismayed.

"We did," he told her gently, "but let's look again."

"A little boy wouldn't be able to reach the pull-down even with the stool."

"No," he agreed and began to climb. "A child wouldn't."

Two bare bulbs overhead cast shadows over the space under the eaves. Lucan stood in the only spot he could, the center, under the sloped roof. Kyra poked her head through the opening and stopped as soon as she saw that the attic was empty. There was nowhere up here for even one child to hide, let alone three of them.

When he turned around, Kyra had disappeared. He found her in the master bedroom. Her head was bowed, her forehead pressed against the glass window. Her posture was one of utter dejection. It tore at him.

As he drew closer he saw the silver tears running silently down her cheeks. He started to back out and give her some privacy but stopped.

Casey Fillmont and her children were Kyra's only close relatives according to the slim dossier he'd compiled on her so far. Their parents had died several years ago. While there were uncles and distant cousins, Kyra had told him they only had each other.

Lucan's own family was tightly knit. He'd be devastated if something ever happened to one of his brothers or their families. Ronan, Neil and Flynn weren't just his brothers, they were his best friends. He loved their wives like sisters and adored his nieces and nephews.

The members of his family were always there for each other. Hadn't Whitney gone out of her way the other day to deliver his mom's lasagna so Lucan could come home to something warm to eat after work? They were always doing things like that. Kyra was alone and frightened. She had no one but him at the moment.

He crossed to where she stood and put his hand on her shoulder in silent support. She turned, wiping furiously at her face.

"No," he told her. "It's okay to cry. Come here."

Lucan drew her into his arms, half surprised when she let him cradle her against his chest. He hadn't bothered to zip his jacket, so it hung open giving her access to his worn flannel shirt. After a few minutes he guided them to the torn-up bed and sat with his back against the headboard. Over her half-hearted protests, he continued to hold her as the tears turned to wrenching sobs.

She'd be embarrassed later, but they'd deal. This was what her body needed at the moment. He liked the light lemony scent of her hair and stroked the silky strands back from her face. It was a measure of her exhaustion that she didn't pull back even when the sobs lessened to shudders that rippled through her.

"Relax," he whispered when she would have raised her head. "It's fine."

And it was. He didn't mind the way his shirt was damp against his skin or the mild cramping caused by his awkward position on the bed. It felt right, holding her this way. Gradually, she relaxed and he let his own eyes close, leaning back against the headboard.

A faint sound opened his eyes. With a start, Lucan realized he'd dozed off. He had no idea how long he'd been sleeping, but he still held Kyra, asleep in his arms. His left arm was badly cramped from her weight. Ignoring the pain, he listened for whatever sound had wakened him. It took his sluggish brain a long moment to recognize what he'd been hearing, and by then the house had fallen silent.

Someone had used the bathroom in the hall. They hadn't closed the door or turned on a light and he waited, hardly breathing, for the sound of a flush. It didn't come, but Lucan knew he hadn't imagined the sound.

Very gently he eased Kyra out of his arms. Instantly, her eyes snapped open. Lucan covered her lips lightly with his fingers, clenching and unclenching his cramped hand. He nodded toward the hall. For someone who'd been asleep only a second ago, she woke quickly and alertly.

As silently as possible, he stood and crossed to the dark hall. The bathroom was empty, but a glance showed he hadn't imagined the sound.

"Where exactly did you see that shadow?" he whispered in her ear.

"Down there, outside the baby's room. He's here, isn't he? Kip's in the house?"

Lucan nodded and stepped into the hall. If the boy had made it back to his hiding spot already, then he was hiding close by.

At the door of the baby's room he listened to the silence a moment before flipping on the light. The room appeared empty, just as it had earlier.

He prowled the small space. There was nowhere for anyone to hide. Unless… He focused on the bookcases. Frowning, he tugged on one, feeling a slight give. He went back to the door and studied the depth of the wall, then met Kyra's excited expression. She'd seen what he was thinking. Inclining his head in tacit agreement, Lucan indicated they should leave the room. He led her back to the master bedroom.

"I knew it!" she whispered excitedly. "I knew he was here somewhere!"

"We should have seen it. There's a panic room behind the bookcases." He gripped her arm when she would have headed back out the door. "Wait. The boy is scared. If he was going to trust you, he would have come out by now. I could force it open, but that would only add to his panic."

"So what do we do?"

"It's almost morning. Most likely, he went back to sleep which means he'll need the bathroom again when he wakes up."

"And he'll be hungry."

Lucan smiled. "Yes. He'll come out if he thinks it's safe. We're going to help him think that it is by staying very quiet."

"He'll run when he sees us."

"We're going to make that tough for him to do. He's smart. He'll realize pretty fast that he has nowhere left to go."

She thought that over. "Thank you, Lucan."

He blinked, surprised by the sound of his first name on her lips. She'd seen his name on his badge and the card he'd given her, of course, but he was pretty sure if she'd thought about it, she would have called him Detective instead. Using his first name implied a level of trust. He liked that thought.

Kyra reddened. "Sorry. I—"

"It's my name. Feel free to use it, but I haven't done anything worthy of thanks just yet."

She wouldn't meet his eyes. "Yes, you have. You didn't arrest me and you even let me cry on your shoulder."

He'd been right. She was embarrassed. "You needed to cry. In your place I would have wanted to cry as well."

She raised her face to meet his eyes. "I can't see you sobbing your heart out on a stranger's shoulder."

"No, I probably would have wanted to hit something instead, but it's the same principal. I'm not a stranger, Kyra. I'm your sister's neighbor and I'm a cop. People cry on our shoulders all the time."

Kyra managed a one-sided smile. He was glad to see the tension leave her features, even if only for an instant.

"All the same, thank you."

"You're welcome. Let's go back in the baby's room and wait for Kip to come out."

KYRA HADN'T EXPECTED TO like the big Irish cop so much, let alone feel this comfortable with him. Dealing in the business world she was always careful to maintain a professional distance with men she met. Simon had claimed it took him three months to get up the courage to ask her out.

She tried to picture Simon offering silent comfort as Lucan had and couldn't. But then, Simon wasn't a touchy-feely sort of guy. She wouldn't have thought Lucan would be either based on their first meeting. That hard-cop exterior hid a surprising well of softer emotions.

And why was she comparing the two men? They were nothing alike. She was so tired that her mind was running in crazy circles.

Shivering, she wished she dared close her eyes for a few more minutes. She jumped and stiffened automatically when Lucan slid his arm around her. He wasn't coming on to her. He held her the way a friend would, offering comfort rather than intimacy. Sitting beside him on the edge of the bed with his broad shoulders pressed against the wall, Kyra realized she trusted Lucan.

She allowed herself to relax and settle back against him. Being touched and held this way was nice. She wondered if Lucan was married and if his wife would be upset if she saw him now. The lack of a wedding ring meant nothing. Many men didn't wear them. But what had his wife thought when he left their bed in the middle of the night to be with another woman?

These were crazy thoughts. Lucan O'Shay was a cop and a nice man. His wife would be a warm, understanding person as well. And she knew thinking about Lucan and his possible wife was a way of keeping her mind from dwelling on what might have happened to Casey.

Her sister had felt so threatened that she'd built a panic room into a house she was renting. How had Kyra not known that?

Milt must have been threatening her again. Casey hadn't said so, but Kyra had known something was wrong when Casey was willing to pull the kids out of school to take a sudden vacation right before Christmas. Casey had refused to explain, but she'd never invited Kyra to go anywhere with her before. When Kyra had asked if Jordan was coming too, Casey had said he couldn't get away.

Maybe Jordan had threatened her, too. Maybe Lucan was right. Maybe Jordan *was* involved in drugs. Kyra knew little about the new man her sister had married. She should never have allowed her life to get so busy that she and her sister were virtual strangers to one another.

With her thoughts tumbling, at first Kyra didn't realize how much easier it was becoming to see objects in the room. Pale shafts of daylight were filtering in through the closed shades on the windows. Lucan hadn't moved. He gave the impression he would sit there like a stone all day if he had to.

What if they were wrong? What if Kip wasn't hiding in the house? What if—

Abruptly, Lucan's muscles tensed. Kyra sat up straight. There were faint rustling sounds and the murmur of a child's querulous voice. Not just Kip! Could all of them be in there?

Lucan stood quietly. He motioned for her to stay put as he closed the door to the hall without a sound. The whispers grew louder, more urgent.

With a gentle snick, the bookcases suddenly parted outward. Kip's eyes went wide with shock and fear when he saw her sitting there. Brian looked startled, but he shook off his brother's hand with a frantic, "I gotta pee!"

Her heart threatened to pound its way through her chest wall, but she managed to keep her voice relaxed and even. "It's okay, Brian. I'm your Aunt Kyra. Go ahead."

He hesitated at the sight of Lucan standing between him and the door.

"That's Lucan. He's a friend."

"Oh."

That was all the confirmation Brian needed. Lucan opened the door and the child scurried out into the hall. Kip didn't move.

Kyra crouched down. "Hi, Maggie. Come here, sweetheart." A dirty tan bear dressed in a gaily colored skirt and vest was clutched to the young girl's chest.

"Mom said not to open the door for anyone," Kip announced belligerently. Fear rippled through his young frame.

Kyra kept her voice low and soothing. "I know. You did the right thing, Kip, but I'm here to help."

"I don't need help."

Maggie looked uncertainly from her brother to Kyra and clutched the bear even tighter. She smelled like she'd had an accident and her bottom lip trembled as if she wasn't sure whether to cry. Kip gripped her small shoulder protectively.

Kyra stood. Keeping her voice brisk and business-like she nodded at the boy, "You've done a fantastic job protecting your brother and sister, Kip. Your mom's going to be very proud of you."

Maggie's lip trembled a bit harder. Tears welled in her eyes. "Mama?"

"I'm Aunt Kyra, Maggie. Everything's going to be all right now."

Kip stared defiance at her.

"I'll bet you're hungry. We have a lot of work to do if we don't want your mom coming home to this messy house. But first, all of you need a bath and some clean clothes."

"And breakfast?" Brian asked coming back in the room.

"Definitely breakfast," Lucan announced drawing Kip's angry gaze back to him. "Kyra, why don't you see to their baths while I make a couple of calls?"

"All right. Kip, you can use your mom's bathroom and I'll take Brian and Maggie in the other one."

"I don't need a bath."

Sympathy would only make him more truculent. "You like smelling like that?"

Brian laughed. "Maggie wet the bed again."

"I can tell. It's your choice, Kip. You're old enough to decide. Come on, Brian. You can show me where things are, right? We'll get cleaned up and go out for pancakes afterwards. How does that sound?"

"Good! Come on, Maggie."

Lucan winked and left the room. Maggie toddled after Brian leaving Kip standing there alone. Kyra longed to hug the defiant child, but knew he would have to come to her on his own terms. She didn't think he'd run away and leave his siblings, so it would be better to give him time to come to terms with her presence. Besides, Lucan was right. Where would he run to?

They were alive and safe. For now, that was enough. She shoved down the dread that filled her at the thought of her sister. Casey would never willingly have left her children alone like this.

Chapter Five

Kyra was nearly as wet as Maggie when she carried the towel-wrapped little girl back into the child's bedroom for some clothes. Kip wasn't there, but she heard water running in the master bathroom and breathed a sigh of relief.

Inside Maggie's hidden closet the children had created what could only be called a nest using blankets, pillows, toys and the food Kip had purchased for them. Her heart ached for what they must have been going through for the past several days. Kyra hadn't asked Brian any questions while she saw to his bath. There would be time enough for that after they were fed and relaxed.

She lightly tickled Maggie as she got her dressed, delighting in the sound of her childish giggles.

"Someone's happy." Lucan filled the doorway.

His smile caused a flutter inside her. "Yes. Would you check on Brian for me?" The words sounded slightly breathless. She hoped he'd put it down to her exertions with Maggie as the child squirmed while she tried to get a shirt over her head.

"I just sent Brian downstairs."

Her head jerked up. "Alone?"

"Of course not. My mom's in the kitchen."

Kyra's jaw dropped. "Your mother?" she parroted. "You called your mother?"

His lips twisted in a wry smile. "She lives nearby. I asked her to bring some supplies over."

"What about your wife?" Kyra snapped her own lips closed too late to prevent the question.

With a slight shrug he turned toward the closet. "I'm divorced."

She was still trying to get her mind around that when he pulled a large red handbag from the depths of the hidden closet. "Your sister's purse?"

Her stomach plunged. Seeing the purse made her sister's plight all the more dire. Horror filling her mind, she watched as Lucan fished out her sister's wallet and confirmed what they both already suspected. There were nine one-dollar bills in the billfold.

Maggie squirmed. Kyra realized she was grasping the child too tightly. She turned her attention back to the little girl, trying to quell her terror.

"I called off the search." He nodded meaningfully toward Maggie. "And I let Captain Walsh know what was happening. Where's Kip?"

"In the master bathroom," she pushed out.

Lucan nodded and returned to the closet. He lifted the battered green backpack and opened the flap. Kyra's eyes widened when she saw the fistful of bills he pulled out.

"I don't understand." But she shivered as more fear crawled down her spine. Had Casey been secreting money to run away?

"Kip dumped his change in the backpack and kept using the large bills I told you about."

Kyra felt numb. "Why?"

"We'll ask him later. To an eight-year-old, money is probably money. I'm guessing it didn't occur to him to use the smaller bills. He wouldn't realize how much attention a boy with a hundred-dollar bill would draw."

"Casey doesn't have that kind of money." She was repeating herself.

Lucan's gaze held sympathy. "Someone did."

Her stomach lurched. "You think Kip stole the money?"

"Possibly."

Maggie had stopped squirming. "Mommy says stealing is bad."

She watched Lucan intently.

"Your mommy's right." He smiled at her. "Let's save this conversation for later, Kyra. I'll want you to count this out with me and sign a release, but I bet Maggie's a hungry little cuddlebear, aren't you sweetheart? I know I am."

Abruptly Maggie's features screwed up. Her head frantically swung around the room. "Bear!"

"We left Bear in the bathroom," Kyra reassured the child. "Come on, let's go find her." Kyra needed to move out of sight of that closet and what it represented. "We'll put your shoes on in there," she soothed the child. Maggie accepted her hand.

Lucan watched them go with a heavy heart. Kyra was right to fear for her sister. He'd give odds that Casey Fillmont was dead. So where had Kip come by all that money? More and more it looked like Casey or her husband were involved in drugs or something else illegal.

He hefted the backpack and followed them from the room. Kip had left the door to the master bathroom open. The shower was running. He heard the boy moving around inside. On the long double vanity next to the door lay a folded, crumpled wad of hundred-dollar bills alongside a rumpled change of clothing.

Lifting the money, Lucan counted twenty-six one-hundred-dollar bills. He was a cop with a cop's instincts. If this didn't turn out to be drug money he was going to be surprised.

The shower stopped. Pocketing the money, Lucan left the room before the boy knew he was there. He couldn't risk Kip taking the cash and running away.

Lucan didn't have long to wait in the hall by the stairs

before Kip came pelting out of the room, his clothes clinging to his still wet body.

"Give me my money," he demanded on the verge of tears as he came to a halt the moment he saw Lucan.

"*Your* money?" The evasive dart of the boy's eyes said it all. "Where did you get the money, Kip?"

"You had no right to take it!"

"Did you?"

Fear swept Kip's young features. His small hands fisted at his sides. Lucan gentled his tone. "I understand, Kip. You had to feed yourself and your brother and sister. Believe it or not, I'm on your side."

Clearly, the boy didn't believe him. Fear had the upper hand and he stood there quivering.

"Tell me what happened."

Kip looked away, blinking hard.

"Your aunt is worried about your mom. We all are."

The boy remained rigidly silent. Lucan sighed. "We want to help you, Kip. All of you."

"Then go away."

He shook his head. "Not going to happen. But you know that. I need to find your mom. She's in trouble, isn't she?"

Sudden tears brimmed in clear blue eyes that reminded him of Kyra's. Lucan ached to comfort the small boy as he had Kyra, but he knew any overture would be spurned. He kept his voice soft.

"Help me help your mom. Tell me what happened."

The boy blinked back his tears and his expression hardened. Lucan wasn't going to reach him. Maybe Kyra would have better luck.

"Okay, Kip. Come downstairs with me. My mom's here making pancakes and sausages. My mom makes terrific pancakes."

"I'm not hungry."

Lucan sighed. "Then you can watch the rest of us eat."

As usual, Maureen O'Shay had cast her Irish charm over the kitchen. Kyra and his mother were working together like longtime friends when Lucan stepped into the fragrant kitchen. Kip followed sullenly in his footsteps and plopped onto the nearest empty chair without looking at anyone.

"Ach, and you should have dried that hair, young Kip," his mother scolded with a gentle smile, "but never you mind. I'm thinking you're as hungry as your brother and sister. I'm Mrs. O'Shay and this brawny man," she gestured at Lucan, "is one of *my* boys. Kyra, some juice for our lads?"

Kyra hastened to pour orange juice into two small glasses. She set one in front of Kip and placed the other at an empty setting before looking at Lucan. He gave a small shake of his head to indicate he'd gotten no answers. She sighed.

"Your mother's a wonder," she told him. "She brought all these supplies with her."

"Lucan told me what was wanting," his mother inserted, returning to the stove to lift a set of fluffy pancakes onto a plate. "It was no trouble at all."

Lucan crossed to kiss the top of her white hair. "Now you see why I called my mother." He poured himself a cup of coffee before taking his seat.

"Do we hafta go back in the closet?" Brian asked his brother.

Kip glared at Lucan as Kyra set the pancakes down in front of him.

"No, Brian," Lucan told him. "No more closet."

Brian nodded and gulped some milk. "Good. When's my mom coming home?"

"As soon as we find her," he told the boy.

"The bad men took her."

Kyra jerked around to stare at the boy with a stricken expression.

"Be quiet," Kip commanded.

"What bad men, Brian?" Lucan asked softly.

"Don't tell him anything!" Kip commanded.

Brian scowled. "Why not?"

"Mom said."

"Did not."

Lucan interrupted. "Did she tell you to stay in the closet?" he asked.

"Uh-huh."

"Shut up!" Kip ordered frantically.

"No! I don't hafta do what you say anymore. Do I, Aunt Kyra? Mom said not to open the door for anyone, but she's been gone a long time. I want her to come home."

Kyra knelt beside him and hugged the boy. "She will, Brian. Lucan's going to find her."

He frowned.

"My Lucan can find her," his mother put in. "And he'll find those bad men and put them in jail where they belong. Don't you fret."

Kip pushed away from the table and ran into the living room. Lucan started to rise but Kyra waved him back.

"I'll go."

"It's been hard on the lad. Let Kyra handle it," his mother suggested.

Reluctantly, Lucan sat back down. He turned to Brian. "Will you tell me what happened?"

The small face showed remembered fear, but he nodded. "The 'lectricity went out, and Mom said we had to get inside the closet and stay there until she told us to come out. She said we had to be quiet no matter what we heard and that Kip was in charge. He wasn't supposed to open the door until she said so." His troubled gaze filled with guilt. "But she didn't come back and I had to go to the bathroom."

"Mommy cried," Maggie put in.

Lucan tensed. He forced himself to relax. "Did she?"

The little girl nodded solemnly and reached for her bear. Her wide eyes held no discernable emotion. "She yelled at the bad men."

"Did you see the bad men?"

Maggie hugged her bear tightly. It was Brian who answered. "No. We was in the closet."

"Do you know how many men there were?"

The boy shook his head. "They made a lot of noise. Mommy kept yelling at them to stop. I wanted to help her but Kip said we had to be real quiet."

"Kip was right, Brian. You did the right thing obeying your mother and staying put." He could see the guilt weighing on the child.

"We were scared. Kip made us stay there even when we couldn't hear anything."

"They made a mess," Maggie pronounced.

"They did indeed," Lucan agreed, meeting his mother's troubled expression. "Did your mom know the men?"

Brian shrugged. Maggie rocked her bear and simply watched.

"Where was your father?"

That brought an immediate reaction. "Daddy doesn't live here," Maggie piped up.

"They got divorced," Brian agreed. "Mom got a new husband, but we don't like him very much."

"Does he hit you?"

His gaze was troubled. "No. Mommy won't let him."

"Does he hit your mother?"

Brian shook his head. "Daddy used to so we ran away."

Even though it was a sadly familiar tale, Lucan tensed. "Was your dad here when the bad men came?"

"Nuh-uh. Jordan called when we got home. Mommy talked to him and got scared. The television turned off all by itself so she made us run upstairs and get in the closet."

Lucan gripped his coffee mug. Had Jordan Fillmont called to warn his wife? Had he known the men were coming?

"What time was this, Brian?"

Brian shook his head.

"Had you eaten dinner yet?"

"Uh-huh. Mom took us to the restaurant where they make tacos."

"Was it dark out when you came home?"

The child stared at him blankly.

"Were there Christmas lights on in the neighborhood?"

"Uh-huh."

That didn't help much in narrowing it down. Kip would be of more help there, assuming Kyra could get him to talk.

"Mama?" Maggie's eyes suddenly filled with tears.

Maureen stepped forward and put her arms around the little girl and her bear. "Your mama will be home soon, little one. Would you be wanting to help me like a big girl? I'm thinking we could bake some cookies to have after lunch. What do you think?"

"Me too?" Brian asked eagerly.

Lucan shot his mother a grateful look.

"Well, of course," she told the child. "Baking cookies means I'll be needing a lot of help."

"What kind of cookies?"

"Well now, what would be your favorite?"

Lucan didn't wait to hear the answer. He stood and crossed to the hall, moving silently into the living room.

"I KNOW YOU'RE SCARED. I'm scared, too, Kip," Kyra told the boy. "But we have to find your mom. We don't want anything bad to happen to her."

Kip remained standing with his back to her. Kyra wondered what she could say to get through to him. It was her own fault he didn't trust her. She should never have let so much time pass without coming for a visit.

"I haven't been a very good aunt, have I? I'm sorry, Kip. I'll try to do better from now on. You did all the right things, but now you have to help Detective O'Shay find your mom."

"I left the closet."

She winced at the guilt in his soft mutter. "That's okay. She didn't mean for you to stay in there for days. You know your mom didn't mean to be gone this long."

He turned around. His expression was far too old for his eight-year-old frame. "Is she going to come back?"

Kyra swallowed hard against the sudden thickening in her throat. She blinked fast to keep tears from filling her eyes. Looking into that young-old face she knew she couldn't lie to him. "I don't know, Kip. But I won't leave you. That, I promise."

She didn't know if he moved or if she did, but she was holding him as he sobbed, wanting to let her own tears fall as well. Her eyes burned, dry and scratchy with need, as her mind whirled with the inconsequential things she needed to do to rearrange her life.

The idea of taking over her sister's role as the children's mother was terrifying. She didn't know how to be a mother. And what was she going to do with three children in her tiny apartment?

They would cope somehow. These fragile lives needed her. She knew what Lucan hadn't said in so many words, what she herself didn't want to think and couldn't stop thinking. Casey was dead. Kyra would have to come to terms with that without shattering. She had children to care for now.

She raised her head to find Lucan watching from the hall. His strong features were sympathetic. Inclining his head, he disappeared back into the kitchen.

After a few minutes, Kip's sobs lessened. He pulled away, wiping furiously at his eyes. "Is Mom dead?"

"I hope not, but I don't know."

He gave an adult nod.

"I do believe Detective O'Shay will do everything he can to find her. But you'll have to help him."

"You look like her. My mom."

Her heart wrenched. "Yes, I do."

"She said we were going to take a vacation with you."

"That was the plan," Kyra agreed gently. "I hope we'll still be able to do that."

He watched her steadily. She didn't want to give him false hope, but she didn't want to crush his hope either. Kip shuddered and sighed. Her heart nearly broke. She had to steady herself before speaking again or she would cry.

"I know you probably aren't hungry, but let's go back in the kitchen and try to eat a little. We can't afford to get sick and we don't want to upset Brian and Maggie. The four of us have to decide what to do next, all right?"

His nod was small, but he let her put her hand on his thin shoulder and walk with him back into the kitchen. Maureen silently placed fresh plates of food in front of them as they joined the others at the table. After one glance at Kyra and Kip, Lucan continued his story about one of his brother's antics when he'd been Brian's age.

Kip said nothing. He didn't look at anyone as he ate with surprising appetite. Kyra barely tasted her food. Her mind continued spinning helplessly.

"Talk to you a minute?" Lucan asked when she put down her fork.

Relieved at a chance to be doing something, she stood and followed him upstairs. Lucan dumped the contents of Kip's backpack on the dresser in the master bedroom. Together they counted out the money. Placing it in an evidence bag, he wrote her a receipt. He gazed at her intently, his cop face firmly in place. "We need to know where he got this."

"I know. But he's a little young for a rubber hose, don't you think?"

His lips pursed. "That wasn't called for."

Kyra sighed. She hadn't meant it to sound like criticism. None of this was his fault and he did have a job to do. "No, it wasn't. I'm sorry."

"Are you willing to take responsibility for the children?"

"Of course I am!"

"There's no 'of course' about it." His tone was mild. "You're a single woman. Having three children will change your life completely. You should take some time to consider a decision of this magnitude."

Angry despite his conciliatory tone, she narrowed her eyes. "My sister isn't dead and buried yet, Detective. And I don't need time to make any decisions. These children are my family."

He smiled then. A full smile. Her lips parted at the re-markable change to his features. How had she not noticed how handsome he was? He took her breath away. His hand rested warmly on her shoulder.

"Besides," she added, unaccountably ruffled, "you'll find Casey."

His body tensed. So did hers. He dropped his hand without commenting.

"What are we going to do about Kip?" she asked to defuse the moment.

His expression changed once more, becoming the cop she had first met. "I have to talk to him, Kyra."

"I know that. I think he feels responsible for what happened."

"That's to be expected. He became the man of the house when his mother put him in charge. Kids have an uncanny knack for thinking things are their fault even when they aren't."

He ran a hand over his unshaven jaw. The stubble gave

him a roguish appearance and she realized how tired he must be. She'd cost him a night's sleep.

"I won't push Kip," he promised. "For one thing, we don't know that this money is tied to anything criminal. And wherever it came from, Kip used it for survival. I need him to talk to me, but I don't browbeat children."

"I know that." And she did. "You're good with kids. I saw the way Brian and even shy little Maggie responded to you." They liked him. So did she. "I'm frustrated because I hate feeling helpless."

His lips curved. "Helpless is one thing I'd never call you."

"Was that a compliment or a complaint, detective?"

His eyes twinkled. He changed the subject without answering. "What are your plans?"

"Long-term?"

"No, now. What are you going to do with the kids today?"

That had been one of many thoughts whirling through her head. She sighed. "I don't know. We can't stay here." She waved her arm at the destruction. "I can't fix this mess completely in a few hours, so I guess I need the name of a motel nearby, in case Casey…" Her throat threatened to close and she swallowed hard. "If she can, she'll come here looking for her kids."

Lucan started to speak and stopped.

"Intellectually I realize she may be dead, Lucan. I do." It was hard to keep the sudden swell of tears from her voice. "But I have to cling to the chance that she's okay."

"There's always a chance," he agreed, despite the doubt filling his eyes. "I have a suggestion. My mother offered to take you and the kids to her place until things get a bit more settled."

The words were so unexpected it took her a minute to process them. "Why? She doesn't even know us."

"My mother has never met a stranger and she loves kids.

A motel is no place for children, especially at this time of year. Mom raised four of us and didn't do a half-bad job. Just don't tell my brothers I said that."

There was deep love and affection behind his words. Kyra was touched by the unexpected offer, and seriously tempted. She'd liked Maureen O'Shay the moment they met.

"It's your decision, of course," he added, "but Mom wouldn't have offered if she didn't want to. She has plenty of room. And I think she's kept every toy we ever had, which should help you keep the kids occupied."

The more Kyra considered the magnanimous offer, the more tempting it was. "We'd be a huge imposition."

"Not really. There's always someone coming by. Mom loves to cook." He rocked back on his heels. "Just think about it, Kyra. What are you going to do with three kids in a motel room all day?"

Good question, and one that seriously worried her. "Kip will want to stay here."

Lucan nodded. He ran a hand through his hair, smoothing back some of the strands that stuck out at odd angles. There hadn't been time this morning for either of them to worry about personal hygiene. Their focus had been on the children. She was suddenly aware of her own bedraggled state. And she had the most outlandish urge to reach out and stroke Lucan's firm jaw.

Their gazes locked. Kyra turned away before she did something utterly stupid. "I'll go talk with your mom."

Chapter Six

Maggie and Brian were excited at the idea of going to Maureen's to make cookies and play with some of the toys Maureen had told them about. Predictably, Kip was upset over leaving the house. He refused to talk with anyone, sitting on the steps with his arms folded and his jaw so tightly shut it made Kyra hurt to look at him.

She plopped down on the step below him. "I don't want to leave, either," she told him quietly.

Kip continued to glare but she could tell he was puzzled. "We have to go for Maggie and Brian."

"Why?"

"Because the furniture's a mess. The beds are torn and there's no place to sleep. I don't think even you want to go back in the closet."

Kip flushed, but set his jaw. "Mom won't know where we are."

His voice broke, taking her heart with it.

"I worried about that, too, but we can leave her a note."

"What if she doesn't see it?"

"We'll tape it to the bookcase outside the closet. That's where she'll go first, don't you think?"

"I guess."

"Why don't you write the note, Kip? Tell her I made us leave because I was afraid the men would come back."

His eyes widened.

"I don't think it's likely, but they could. We'll write down Mrs. O'Shay's address and phone number so your mom will know how to reach us."

He shook his head. "If the men come back, they might see it."

Out of the mouths of babes.

"Good point. We'll just tell your Mom you're with me. She knows my cell phone number, so we won't have to write that down." She patted his knee. "I need you, Kip. You're the man of the family right now. Maggie and Brian may get scared if we don't come home tonight. You have to be with me to keep them calm. They trust you, but they hardly know me. Will you help?"

He thought about it for long seconds. "I guess."

"Thanks. We'll start packing what you need for a couple of days. Hopefully by then the police will have found your mom."

"Maggie will want her bear dresses."

"Bear dresses?"

"She likes to dress Bear in different outfits. She never goes anywhere without Bear."

Kyra relaxed. It was going to be okay. "See, this is why I need you. Does the bear have a name?"

"Just Bear. Can I take my gamer?"

"Absolutely." Having spent hours in the toy store choosing the gifts she'd brought, she knew the handheld game device was the current rage for the preteen set.

She was stuffing the last of Maggie's bear costumes into the pillowcase she was using for a suitcase when she tripped on a toy and banged her ankle on the edge of the metal bed frame. Hissing in pain, she swore under her breath and grimaced, closing her eyes. She could feel her ankle throb beneath the soft leather of her boot. When she opened her eyes again, Kip was standing there holding his own pillow-case with a frightened expression on his small face.

"It's okay, Kip. I just bumped my ankle. I'm fine." She rubbed the appendage, finding torn leather where she'd hit.

"Aunt Kyra, are the police going to put me in jail?"

All thoughts of her bruised ankle and her sister fled. "No. Of course not."

"Even if I did something bad?"

Fear tickled her stomach. "Not even then. I'm a lawyer, you know."

"For real?"

"For real. Are you worried because of the money?"

He nodded and wouldn't meet her eyes. "That man wants to know where I got it."

Kyra saw "that man" standing in the doorway behind Kip. Freshly shaven, Lucan wore a dark suit that empha-sized the breadth of his wide shoulders. He'd gone home at some point, showered, shaved and changed clothes. He wore a long, heavy coat, unbuttoned. The temperature outside must have dropped.

Kyra didn't think Kip knew Lucan was there, so she tried not to look directly at him. Hunkering down, she put herself at the boy's level and took his hand.

"If I'm going to be your lawyer, Kip, you need to tell me everything. I won't let anyone arrest you no matter where you got the money. I promise."

"I can't pay it back."

"That's okay. I can if we need to."

His dark, troubled eyes stared into hers. He nodded, set his pillowcase down and turned toward the closet. Kyra shared a quick glance with Lucan who nodded encourag-ingly. She limped after Kip. The boy tugged aside the nest of smelly blankets until the carpeted floor showed.

Kyra watched as he used a toy figurine to pry back the baseboard. Shoving his hand into the surprisingly long gap he exposed, he pulled out a plastic bag. Even before he held it out to her, she saw what appeared to be more money inside.

"I took it from here," he told her.

"Oh." The word escaped on a breath of surprise. The bills were all one-hundred-dollar denomination. And there were a lot of them.

"Kip, how did this money get here?"

"I don't know." He shrugged. "Brian found it when his toy got stuck in that board. All the food was messed up downstairs and Mom only had a little money in her purse, so I had to take some of this so I could go to the store. We were hungry."

Kyra pulled him against her in a hug. "You did exactly right," she told him fiercely, thinking how frightened they must have been. "You had to take care of your brother and sister."

"But the police will arrest me 'cause I stole the money."

"No. We won't, Kip."

Startled, they both turned at the sound of Lucan's deep soothing voice.

"Your aunt is right. You did what you had to do. You're a brave guy. I'm not sure I would have been half as brave at your age. Do you know where this money came from?"

Kip shook his head.

"Is it okay if I take the rest? I'll count the money and give your aunt a receipt like I did with the money from your backpack. We have to see if we can find out who it belongs to."

It was as if a weight had been lifted from Kip's fragile shoulders. "Okay. She's my lawyer. I can trust her."

Lucan's eyes crinkled with humor. "You're right. She's a fierce lawyer. Why don't you take your pillowcase downstairs while I talk to your aunt?"

"Okay."

Lucan turned to her as soon as the boy left the room. "Why are you limping?"

"The bed frame and my ankle had a disagreement. I lost."

"You should take those sexy boots off."

He thought her boots were sexy?

"Do you want me to look at it?"

She pictured his large warm hands caressing her ankle and a quiver went through her.

"It's fine," she told him hurriedly. "We should count the money."

"Kyra. Let's see the foot first. You don't want it to swell inside that leather. Sit down over here and let me take it off. Don't be a wimp."

Her chin came up. "I am *not* a wimp."

"Then let me have a look."

Seeing no graceful way out of it, she perched on the edge of the baby's bed. "I can take it off," she told him as he reached for her leg, gently extending it.

"Let me."

It was only a boot, she told herself. There was nothing romantic in a man holding her leg and peeling her out of a boot. So why did the feel of his hand seem so erotic? The zipper was unnaturally loud as he parted it with almost sensual care.

"You're enjoying this," she charged.

"Of course I am. I've always had a foot fetish," he deadpanned.

At least, she thought he was teasing. "You *are* kidding, right?"

He winked and slid the boot slowly from her foot. She tried not to squirm as he set it aside and began to peel her long sock down her skin. She was embarrassed and achingly aware of how sexy Lucan was.

Lucan was being incredibly gentle so he didn't hurt her.

Any and all sexual vibes were strictly coming from her imagination.

Weren't they?

The sock came free. He set it on the bed, cupping her heel in one warm palm while he probed the swollen appendage gently with the fingers of his other hand.

"It doesn't feel like you broke anything, but I hope you brought along a pair of flat shoes."

Her cheeks were hot as he stroked the swollen skin. "I have running shoes in my bag."

"You're a runner?"

"Yes."

"So am I." He looked inordinately pleased and turned his attention back to her ankle. "It may bruise." His thumb rubbed the side of her foot and her breathing caught. She'd never realized how sensitive her feet were before. His face was so close, and she watched his eyes darken to a deep, sensual gray. The scent of his light spicy cologne was heady.

Was he going to kiss her?

Was she going to let him?

"Ach, no. You canna be taking your entire room along with you, young Brian."

At the sound of his mother's voice, Lucan released her foot and stood, breaking whatever spell had held them in thrall. "Stay there while we count out this money."

Her imagination must be on overdrive. Good thing he couldn't read her crazy thoughts. He dumped the bills on the torn bed and began to count them out.

"Nearly eighteen thousand dollars?" She stared at him, appalled.

"Plus what Kip already took out. There may be more in the wall. I'm going to have to have a team in here taking a thorough look."

She could barely speak. "This has to belong to Jordan. Casey never had this kind of money."

"Brian says Fillmont called Casey when they got home on Sunday after dinner. The power went out, and she made them all go upstairs and get in the closet. That must be when the phone line was cut. We checked with the Oak Forest Country Club. No one has seen Fillmont since Saturday afternoon. He had Sunday off, but he didn't show up for work on Monday."

"He's missing, too?"

"Looks that way. Why don't you find another pair of shoes while I go talk to my office."

"Fine."

"Oh, and Kyra? Has anyone ever told you that you have very sexy feet?"

He was out the door with a little-boy grin before she could think of a thing to say. Kyra removed her other boot and sock with fingers that shook. She was so going to pay him back for that.

By the time she took a quick shower and changed clothes, Lucan was gone. Several other officers had arrived. She spoke with Maureen, cleared it with the officer in charge and headed to her car accompanied by Kip.

Maureen had decided to take the younger two with her to the grocery store. Kip opted to go to the mall with Kyra instead. They were leaving the house to the police.

Kyra noticed a car down the street pull away from the curb when she left the driveway. So Lucan had decided she needed a babysitter. She should have been annoyed, but the gesture was actually reassuring. Hopefully he had someone watching his mom and the other children as well. The driver maintained enough distance that he was an indistinct shape.

Glancing over at Kip, she wondered if it was Kip they were watching. Lucan probably didn't trust her nephew not to run away again. But he wouldn't. She was sure of it. He was more relaxed now that he knew he wasn't going to be arrested. He sat beside her, fascinated by the GPS system leading them to the nearest mall. She really needed more clothes than she'd brought with her, including another pair of boots.

The parking lot was packed, but she lucked into a front-row space near Macy's. The police officer, she decided, was on his own. She wasn't waiting for him. Kip waited patiently as she made short work of her purchases.

"I didn't know you had a gamer system," she told her nephew, "but I think you more than earned a new game for taking such good care of your siblings. Want to pick one up while we're here?"

His expression brightened and just as quickly clouded. "No. That's okay."

Sensing where his thoughts had gone she held his gaze. "It's okay, Kip. Your mom wouldn't want you to sit around and brood until Lucan finds her. Help me pick out something for your brother and sister as well."

"Okay. Maggie's easy. She likes clothes and stuff for Bear."

Kip had no problem pointing out things for Brian as well. Kyra was paying for the items when Kip tugged on her arm. He lowered his voice, looking scared. She had to bend down to hear him.

"Aunt Kyra, there's a man staring at us."

Following his gaze, she saw a tall man turn abruptly away from the front window of the store. Something in his furtive movement sent a chill straight down her spine. Her hand shook as she signed the credit slip the clerk handed her.

"Excuse me, but do you have a bathroom I could use?"

"There's public restrooms down—"

She shook her head at the teenager's implacable expression. "Never mind."

She nudged Kip. "I forgot something. Come with me."

He followed as she hurried to the back of the crowded store. There was an Employees Only door and she pushed it open, striding inside a dark stockroom area.

"What are you doing, Aunt Kyra?"

"We're going to find the back way out of here. Come on."
She prayed an alarm wouldn't sound as she hurried through
the cluttered room to the door at the far end.

"I don't think we're supposed to be here, Aunt Kyra."

"I know. Hurry, Kip."

Nothing sounded as she pushed that door open. A dimly
lit corridor extended in two directions with exit doors at
either end. Kyra turned left. She figured the right passage
would lead back into the mall and was rewarded when her
choice opened onto an asphalt loading area and the store's
trash bins.

"Where are we going?" Fear pitched his voice high and
reedy.

"It's okay, Kip." Beyond the loading area was the parking
lot, but they were nowhere near where they had parked.
"We're going over there."

"Over there" was another mall entrance. The sight of
people coming and going and milling about was reassuring.
All they had to do was locate mall security and call Lucan.
If she was overreacting and the man had been a cop, she'd
give Lucan a dressing down he wouldn't soon forget for
scaring them.

She rushed Kip across the tarmac, ignoring a twinge from
her sore ankle. The child had to run to keep up with her, but
she knew the man outside the toy store wouldn't be stopped
by her ploy for long. And if he wasn't one of Lucan's people…

A gust of cold air swept over them. Kyra didn't look
back until they reached the mall entrance. When she did,
she was in time to see the man emerge from the loading
area and scan the parking lot. She knew the minute he
spotted them. Her view was instantly cut off by a passing
crowd but it was enough. She wasn't overreacting. That guy
was no cop.

There was a movie theater on their right as they stepped

back inside the mall. A crowd of young teenagers nearly filled the wide mall corridor. The aroma of popcorn wafted on the air. A long line of mostly teens waited to purchase tickets.

"In here, Kip."

"We're going to a movie?" His voice shook. She was scaring him.

"No, we're going to call Detective O'Shay."

"Is that man following us?"

She wished she could lie. He was so young and so scared. "I think so. Stay with me. Don't get separated, okay?"

"Okay." He gripped the bag he was carrying more tightly.

She bypassed the line and opened the door, pausing in front of the young ticket collector. "I need your manager," she told the girl in her most officious tone. "It's an emergency."

"Uh…"

"Where's his office?"

"Behind the concession stand. But you need a ticket."

Kyra leveled a hard stare at the girl. "No, I don't." She pushed past and wove her way to the concession stand. A six-foot poster for an upcoming movie put them out of direct line of sight of the door.

The concession stand was doing a brisk business. Kyra hesitated long enough to spot the opening in the counter. She hurried over to it. The moment she lifted the hinged top a scrawny youth looked up. "Hey, you can't come back here."

"I need to see the manager."

"He's not here."

Unlike the ticket collector, this boy planned to stand his ground. He stepped in front of her with determination.

"I'll get the assistant manager for you. Wait there."

Kyra would have argued, but the boy crossed to the door at his back and opened it. Without taking his gaze from her he called out. "Mr. Garber, a lady out here wants to see you."

A skinny, balding man hurried forward, looking annoyed. The tiny sign on his shirt designated him as the assistant manager.

"May I help you?"

Kyra lowered her voice. "We need security right away. There's a man following us. He may be armed."

That got the officious little twerp's attention. His eyes widened. He looked behind her. Kyra elbowed her way past him into what passed for an office.

"Shut the door," she ordered, dropping her packages and fishing in her purse for her cell phone and Lucan's card.

"You can't be back here," the man squeaked.

Kip closed the door, but not before Kyra glimpsed their pursuer pushing his way past the ticket taker and inside the theater lobby. She didn't think he had seen them.

"What do you think you're doing? I'm calling security."

"Good. I'm calling the police."

His mouth snapped shut. He scurried behind a cluttered desk where the remains of a fast-food hamburger and French fries told her she'd interrupted his lunch. He lifted a phone. Kyra ignored him, punching in Lucan's number. She couldn't control the erratic beat of her heart, but she did try to control her panicked breathing. One ring. Two. Three.

She swore softly, ignoring the sound of the assistant manager's voice squeaking into the phone.

"Pick up!" she demanded of Lucan.

"Lucan O'Shay."

Kyra let go a gust of relief. "It's Kyra."

His tone sharpened. "What's wrong?"

"Did you have police officers following us to the mall?"

"No." His voice turned to gravel. "Where are you?"

"In the manager's office at the movie theater. He's calling security."

"Is Kip with you?"

"Yes. Kip saw a man watching us in the toy store. The man followed us inside the lobby of the theater."

"Okay, stay there. See if you can lock the door. I'll have uniformed officers there in a minute. I'm on my way."

He disconnected and she closed the phone. Funny how reassured his last words made her feel.

The assistant manager watched her with growing excitement. It changed to fear as she clicked the lock into place despite the fact that the feeble thing wouldn't keep out a ten-year-old.

"Security's on the way." His strained voice betrayed his growing panic.

"Good. So are the police. Is there another way out of here?"

"No." He swallowed convulsively.

Under the permeating scent of popcorn, Kyra could smell the greasy odor emanating from his food.

"Is he dangerous?"

"Yes," she agreed shortly. "Kip, get under the desk."

"Ohmigod." The man looked frantically around the room as if seeking another exit.

"What about you?" Kip protested.

"I'll be fine." The man must want Kip and the money.

"But—"

"Kip!" Reluctantly, he moved beside the now-terrified assistant manager and slipped down out of sight.

The room was a trap. Unfortunately, it was too late to make other choices. Kyra opened her purse. Her hand closed over her gun. Useless. Lucan still had the bullets, and she certainly didn't want to fire it in a theater filled with teenagers. She held it out while digging for the pepper spray.

"Omigod! Ohmigod!" The little man's eyes threatened to bulge out of his head. "Don't shoot me! Please don't shoot me! I have a dog! She's going to have puppies in a few days!"

"Congratulations." If it hadn't been so pathetic his words would have been funny. She was afraid he might faint. "Sit down."

He collapsed on the seat of his chair like a deflated balloon. The sudden sharp rap on the door made them all jump. He was back on his feet once more.

"Mr. Garber? Security's here."

Kyra pulled out the pepper spray. There was no way to tell if the kid was being coerced by the man who was looking for them.

"Tell security to wait out there until the police arrive," she whispered to the terrified assistant manager.

He trembled so hard she was sure he'd pass out. His voice quaked, but he parroted her words.

"Uh, Mr. Garber, are you okay?"

Kyra gave the teen credit. Unlike his manager, the youth had good instincts. She glared at Garber, willing him to speak.

"Yes," he squeaked.

The boy began speaking to someone. The youth sounded calm, but worried. She doubted his tone would be so even if their pursuer was standing there with him. Still, she held the pepper spray ready to give anyone coming through that door a nasty surprise.

"This is Wilmott from Security, Mr. Garber. Are you okay in there?"

"Yes." His Adam's apple bobbed frantically in his long, thin neck. With a wild glance at Kyra he added defiantly, "Call the police."

Kyra nodded. Obviously puzzled, he gaped at her. There was a squawk on the man's radio on the other side of the door. His voice was too low a rumble to be understood as he responded.

"Sir, the police are already on the way."

Garber's expression was triumphant. Kyra smiled at him.

For the first time she relaxed a bit. But she didn't put her pepper spray back in her purse until there was another, solid rap on the door minutes later.

"Police. Open the door."

Chapter Seven

Lucan arrived to find Kyra sitting behind a scarred old desk in the manager's chair. She appeared calm and unruffled despite the hands cuffed behind her back. A wide-eyed, silent Kip stood close beside her. Until that moment, Lucan hadn't noticed how strong the resemblance was between them. She could have been Kip's mother instead of his aunt.

They looked up as he entered the small, crowded room. Lucan motioned the uniformed officer outside. "Handcuffs?"

"The woman was carrying concealed," the officer announced.

"You searched her?"

"After the assistant manager alerted us."

"Okay. Wait out here." He entered and looked from her to the boy. "Hey, Kip. Are you all right?"

He nodded and if anything, moved even closer to Kyra. "Are they going to arrest us?"

"No."

"Then would you get me out of these?" Kyra asked.

"I don't know. It seems to me keeping you under lock and key might be the only way to keep you out of trouble. What do you think, Kip?"

The hunch of the boy's shoulders relaxed a fraction.

Lucan winked at him and walked over to release the cuffs. "I'm starting to think you have a thing for these."

Kyra offered a mock scowl. "I prefer mine velvet-lined with a quick release."

He quirked a grin at her unexpected riposte. She rubbed her wrists.

"I'll remember that," he promised. "I did warn you that I didn't want to see that gun again."

"Not my fault." She shrugged. "The assistant manager saw it when I got the pepper spray out. He told the officers about the gun when I opened the door."

"So I was told. What exactly happened?"

"You tell him," she urged Kip. "He'll believe *you.*"

Surprised, Kip hesitatingly began to recount the events. Kyra nodded agreement when he finished.

"Okay. Thanks, Kip. Let's get out of here. My mother is waiting lunch on us."

"As long as it isn't a hamburger," she told him, eyeing the congealing, pungent food sitting on the desk in front of her.

"Yeah," Kip agreed, making a face.

"What about my gun?" she asked.

"I'll hold on to it for awhile, unless you want to meet the entire force, one by one." Her glower reminded him of his mother's.

"And my pepper spray?"

He handed her the small canister the officer had given him, then helped Kip gather up their bags.

"I'll carry those for you."

"We can manage."

"Beyond a doubt, but why not let me play mule?"

She smiled fully. "When you put it that way—load him up, Kip."

Kip's face lit in a real smile for the first time. Kyra gave Lucan a grateful glance as Kip handed over the rest of the packages.

The assistant manager stood outside the door behind the concession stand when they exited. He eyed them sourly. Kyra paused to address him. "Sorry for all the trouble. Good luck with your puppies."

The man's face reddened and he turned away.

"What was that all about?" Lucan asked.

"His dog's pregnant," Kip volunteered.

Kyra merely shrugged, crossing to where Todd stood with the two uniforms. "Detective Berringer. I didn't realize you were here, too."

"I was with Lucan when you called."

"Sorry I had to interrupt."

"No problem. Are we set?" he asked Lucan.

"Good to go. Thanks, guys." The uniforms nodded and moved off. Lucan turned to Kyra. "Where are you parked?"

"Almost directly in front of Macy's."

"Give Todd your keys and he'll follow with your car. You and Kip can ride with me."

She met his gaze. Understanding flashed in her expression. Kyra realized what he didn't want to say in front of Kip. There was a possibility her car was being watched. She handed over her keys with a word of thanks to Todd.

"Sure you don't want to go for X-rays on that ankle?" he asked as she limped beside him.

"Positive. It's just bruised. It's going to hurt for a few days, that's all."

Her cell phone rang as they reached the car. She groaned as she saw the caller ID. "Excuse me a minute. If I don't take this, he'll just keep calling." Looking away, she answered her phone. "Simon? What's up?" She slid a glance at Lucan. He made a point of turning around to be sure Kip was buckled in.

"You aren't! Dulles? Why?" A faint blush stained her cheeks. Lucan started the car, wishing he could hear more than the rumble of a man's voice.

"That's very nice of you, but…" Her color deepened. She slid another glance his way.

"Simon, I can't! I'm staying with someone." She clutched the phone more tightly.

Lucan decided right then that he didn't like Simon.

"No. Simon. Simon!"

Obviously, Simon had disconnected. Lucan had seen Kyra stressed and upset, but he'd never seen her rattled before. She was rattled now. She wouldn't meet his eyes and she picked her words with care.

"That was…a friend of mine. He's coming to town. He wants to help."

"How?" Lucan asked flatly.

"I have no idea." She closed her eyes and rubbed her forehead with a fist. "You'll like him." Her voice was flat. "Everyone does."

Lucan doubted that. "My mother's house only has three empty bedrooms," he cautioned her, aware of Kip listening in the back seat.

"Oh, don't worry, he'll stay in a hotel."

Alone? he wanted to ask. "This Simon have a last name?"

"Testier. Simon Testier. He works with me at Dowling."

"So he's a lawyer, too?"

She shook her head. "He's strictly recovery. When art or jewelry or whatever one of our clients has insured goes missing, it's our job to recover the item or arrange for its return."

"In other words, you're both insurance investigators."

She frowned. "What we do is somewhat unique."

"Uh-huh." He was going to run a check on both Simon Testier and Dowling Limited. After all, there could be a connection to what Kyra did for a living and her sister's disappearance somehow.

"So Testier is a close friend of yours?"

She shifted uncomfortably. That was answer enough.

Someone as smart and attractive as Kyra was bound to have a lover.

"You might want to warn him about carrying concealed," he added before she could respond to his question.

"He's flying in from Germany on a commercial flight. We don't carry weapons on planes. You won't need your handcuffs."

"You never know." He could always hope.

THE AROMA OF BAKING chocolate and vanilla laced with cinnamon filled his mother's house. She greeted Kyra like an old friend and hustled her and Kip upstairs along with the other two children to select bedrooms.

Todd arrived a short time later with Kyra's car. He inhaled deeply and smiled blissfully. "I love your mother. If I thought she'd have me, I'd propose just to come home to smells like this every day."

"Don't even go there or I'll shoot you with your own gun."

Todd made a face. "You don't know how good you have it. My mother's so health-conscious, the last time she baked cookies was two years ago. Tell me we're going to stay for lunch," Todd pleaded.

Kyra started down the stairs. Lucan turned to watch her. "We're going to stay for lunch."

"I don't think she's on the menu," Todd whispered.

Lucan glared a warning. "Her boyfriend's on his way to Dulles as we speak." As she approached he asked in a normal tone, "Any trouble in the parking lot?"

Todd didn't miss a beat. "Nope. No watchers I could spot and no one tailed me."

"I'm not sure that's good. I'd like to know what they wanted."

"Probably the money Kip found," Kyra pointed out.

"How would they know he found it?"

"Maybe the same way you did."

Lucan considered. It was possible the men had been looking for the children as potential witnesses, but it didn't feel right.

"We'll go have a talk with the manager at the golf club after lunch," Lucan told Todd.

His friend shook his head. "Walsh wants me back on the Nestler woman's murder and the Fisk robbery. I need to interview the dead woman's housekeeper again and talk to some of Fisk's neighbors. You're on your own this afternoon."

"I can go with you," Kyra offered.

"This is police business," Lucan replied.

"Doesn't your police department have a citizen's ride-along program?"

"That's for uniforms, not detectives."

She raised her eyebrows. "I might be able to help."

"You have a *friend* coming, remember?"

Her eyes narrowed. Todd interjected. "You shouldn't be driving around town on your own right now, Ms. Wolf-stead. Since you were followed to the mall, someone knows your car. Your out-of-state plate's too easy to spot."

"Todd's right. You need to stay out of sight until we can figure out what's going on. I'm going to see about putting your car in my mother's garage."

The light of battle gleamed in her eyes. Fortunately, his mother came down the steps before she could retort.

"Hello, Todd, I thought I heard your voice."

"Mrs. O'Shay, it's good to see you again."

"Where are the kids?" Lucan asked.

"The lads are checking out the air hockey game."

Todd's expression lit up. "Your mom has an air hockey game?"

"It used to be mine."

His mother beamed at Todd. "You'll be staying for lunch then. It will be ready in five minutes. You lads go and wash up while I set another place."

"I'll give you a hand, Maureen," Kyra offered with a glare that let Lucan know they'd be having words when she got him alone.

The women disappeared into the kitchen. Lucan turned to find Todd watching him. "She's a looker."

"She's part of a case."

"Keep telling yourself that."

"Go wash your hands."

Todd looked smug as he headed for the tiny hall bathroom. Lucan was annoyed that his attraction to Kyra was so transparent. He barely admitted it to himself. He liked her sense of humor and her ability to think on her feet, and she *was* attractive. Far too attractive for his comfort level.

He banished the memory of holding her soft foot in his hand because that was just weird. He'd never been turned on by a foot before. Yet he'd nearly kissed her.

And she would have let him. The attraction wasn't all one-sided. But she had a boyfriend and he had a job to do. Once this case was concluded he'd never see her again.

The knowledge was depressing.

LUCAN WAS USHERED INTO the impressive main office of the Oak Forest Country Club where a well-tailored man rose to greet him.

"Detective O'Shay, I'm Louis Ventner, the general manager. How may I help you?"

"Mr. Ventner. I'd like to speak with Jordan Fillmont."

The man had a great poker face. "Frankly, Detective, so would I. I assume this has to do with his missing wife?"

So far they had managed to keep the details from the media, but they'd released the fact that Casey was missing and sent out a photograph. The burglary and murder of wealthy heiress Shereen Nestler still had most of the media attention along with most of the force's manpower, so he wasn't surprised that Ventner knew about Casey.

"When was the last time you saw Mr. Fillmont?"

"I personally spoke with him on Saturday morning. Jordan ran our pro shop. He booked tee times, scheduled our golf, tennis and fitness pros, maintained inventory at the shop and that sort of thing. He's a personable man, which made him popular with our members. Until Saturday afternoon I would have called him an exemplary employee."

Lucan noted his use of past tense. "What changed on Saturday afternoon?"

Ventner paused to consider before speaking. "According to Alice—that's Alice Drubowski, she works with him on weekends—according to her, Jordan abruptly announced he was feeling ill and left. Calls to his cell phone and home telephone have gone unanswered since then."

Lucan paused to consider. "Did Mr. Fillmont handle money for your club?"

Ventner's gaze narrowed. "Only the cash register in the pro shop. We have an accounting department that handles our main finances."

"I take it Mr. Fillmont won't be welcomed back?"

Venture leaned forward. "Not without a superior excuse. No, Detective, he won't be welcomed back. Does he have a superior excuse?"

"As soon as I find him, I'll let you know. Would it be possible for me to speak with Ms. Drubowski?"

"Of course." He hit an intercom button on his telephone. "Ralph, ask Robby to cover the pro shop and have Alice report to my office immediately, please."

"Yes, sir."

Alice Drubowski was an athletic-looking middle-aged woman with a wide, friendly smile that displayed a set of crooked front teeth.

"Jordan's easy to work with," she told Lucan. "Everyone likes to stop by and chat with him. That's part of his job, but he's exceptionally good at it."

"Does he pay more attention to, say, the female members than—?"

"No, sir. Nothing like that. He never crosses the line, even with the young ones who like to flirt. Mr. Ventner wouldn't stand for it and neither would I. Jordan asks members how their game went, how their families are doing and what's new in their lives. You know, routine things."

Lucan nodded. "What happened on Saturday, Ms. Drubowski?"

"Well, that was odd, I can tell you." She frowned. "We'd been real busy and hit a lull. Jordan looked out the window and got this horrified expression on his face. He turned to me and said, 'Alice, I need to leave, I'm sick,' then he bolted out the back door. I thought he ate something that disagreed with him."

"Did he look ill?"

"Yes, sir, he did. He was real pale. Bill—that's Bill Jaff, our golf pro—came in with some new guy he was showing around and I asked him to check on Jordan when he got back to the main building. That's where I thought he'd gone, because the pro shop doesn't have a bathroom."

"Was Mr. Fillmont looking at Mr. Jaff or anyone else in particular when he stared out the window?"

"I couldn't say. I remember he waved to the Cassios and the Martins. Mr. Markham and his partner were walking past on their way to the tennis courts. There were a lot of people out there, Detective. Saturday was a gorgeous day and the club was busy. All this unseasonable air has brought people out."

"You're open all year around?"

"Yes, sir. Is it true Mr. Fillmont's wife is missing, too?"

Lucan nodded. "Did anything unusual happen right before Mr. Fillmont left?"

"Not really. We had to call the new greens keeper over to fix the flower bed outside the shop after Mrs. Liu ran over it in her golf cart again, but that happens pretty regularly. You'd think they'd just take it out, but it is pretty, even at this time of year. They change the plants with the season, you know."

"And the greens keeper is new? Had Mr. Fillmont met him before?"

"I couldn't say. It was the first time I'd seen him, and he didn't last."

Lucan's interest perked. "He's not here any longer?"

"No, he quit the next day. Didn't even bother coming in." Curiosity gleamed in her eyes.

Lucan changed track. "What about the person your golf pro was showing around? Did he join?"

"Oh, I've no idea. You'd have to ask Mr. Ventner."

"Is that typical? The golf pro showing someone around?"

"No, usually Ralph or Sara would do that, but if they're busy, one of us fills in. We're pretty flexible around here."

Lucan felt certain Jordan Fillmont had seen something, or more likely some*one* who had caused his hasty departure on Saturday. He thanked her and went looking for others to speak with. Everyone liked Fillmont. And everyone was dying of curiosity.

Fillmont had left the pro shop at three thirty-two according to Alice Drubowski, yet he hadn't called his wife until she and the children had returned home after dinner. Where had he been in the interim? And where was he now?

KYRA STARED AT THE computer screen, her fingernails absently tapping the desktop. She'd selected the smaller bedroom because it had a desk and a plug for her computer. Once Maureen shooed her out of the kitchen, she'd gone to work.

Jordan Fillmont had lived a squeaky-clean existence until two years ago. Too clean. Not only was there no trace of drugs or a criminal record, he'd never had so much as a parking ticket until two years ago. Now he had not one but six tickets, plus two speeding tickets, two warnings and a drunk-and-disorderly-conduct arrest with the charges dismissed. His on-line résumé claimed he'd managed a men's wear store—now out of business—and prior to that a sporting good store, also defunct. Kyra couldn't find any record of the man dating back more than two years.

Her cell phone rang and she opened it, still staring at the computer screen.

"Kyra? Where are you?"

Simon Testier's voice was a cold shot of water to the face. "Simon?"

"Of course it's Simon. I'm at the airport. Where are you?"

"Busy."

"You aren't picking me up?" He managed to sound hurt.

"No, Simon. I'm not picking you up."

"You're still mad. I'll get a cab."

"Get a flight to Boston instead. I don't have time to deal with you right now, Simon."

His voice gentled in that suave, soothing manner that had once captivated her. "Your sister is still missing, right? I can help."

Kyra hesitated. She knew there was a chance he *could* help. Hadn't she nearly called him earlier? Simon was a suave manipulator, but he was also a top-notch investigator.

"I got the message, babe. I know you want some distance, but this is special. Let me help. Where are you?"

She was going to regret this, she just knew it. "I'm staying with Casey's children at a friend's house."

"I didn't know you had close friends in the D.C. area."

Kyra didn't respond.

"Right. Give me the address. I'll take a hotel room and pick you up for dinner about seven."

"The children need to eat earlier than that, Simon," she told him mock-sweetly. "And they prefer fast food. Make it six." She recited the address and closed her cell phone with a satisfying snap. Simon hated fast food. She suspected he wouldn't much care for young children, either.

Lips curving upward, Kyra turned off her cell phone before he could call back. Maybe something in this situation would work out to her advantage.

LUCAN'S THOUGHTS TUMBLED as he drove. At the last minute, he changed his mind and veered toward his mother's. He hadn't questioned the children in depth. Maybe Kip would know if Jordan had been acting odd lately.

Lucan dismissed the stray thought that he just wanted another excuse to see Kyra.

He was only a few blocks away when he heard a call come in over the radio and recognized the address. An officer was in foot pursuit of a subject fleeing the Fillmont house. Lucan made a quick U-turn. He followed the pursuit on his radio so he knew when the suspect made it to a green four-door sedan.

Lucan saw the car minutes later as it sped up a narrow residential street. There wasn't time to think and plan. The driver came around a corner right at him at a ridiculous rate of speed. Trees lined the street on one side, parked cars on the other. There was no time to plan and nowhere for either of them to go once the other driver lost control.

Lucan tried to turn aside, knowing it was hopeless. A detached part of his mind registered the fear on the driver's face a second before his sedan slammed into the passenger's side of Lucan's unmarked police car.

The impact threw his head against the side window with enough force to close his eyes. When he forced them open seconds later, his car was on the sidewalk. The driver's door was wedged against the bole of a maple tree. Blood trickled down his face, blurring his vision, but he saw Jordan Fillmont running from the scene.

Even as the welcome sound of approaching sirens filled the air, Lucan realized he wasn't getting out of what was left of the car without some help. Then everything went black.

Chapter Eight

Lucan looked up as the curtains on the hospital cubicle parted once more. His brother Ronan's wife, Sally, looked him up and down with a critical nurse's eye.

"Honestly, between you and your brother Flynn, we're going to have to start setting aside an ER cubicle just for the O'Shay men. Or did you total your unit so you could come here and flirt with Tina?"

"Who?"

Her expression softened. "The nurse I introduced you to the other day. Never mind. You know, I used to worry about being married to a pilot. Now I'm just glad he isn't a cop or a fireman. Why couldn't you all be lawyers like your brother Neil?"

"My mother asks that question every day."

Sally laughed. "Dr. Phanlo says your head is rock-hard, but you do have a mild concussion and you're going to feel every one of those lovely bruises come morning."

"Do you know if they caught the guy who hit me?"

She shook her head. "You can ask Todd and your captain. They're outside along with a very stunning young woman named Kyra."

Lucan jerked and winced as all sorts of muscles protested. "Kyra's here?"

His sister-in-law's expression was knowing. "Uh-huh. Your mother sent her."

He groaned. "Mom knows I'm here?"

"Yep. And since I've seen for myself that you'll live, I need to get back upstairs." She paused to smile at him. "Maureen is excited to have Kyra and the children staying with her. I'm glad you suggested it. They're good for her. She's decided to put up a Christmas tree this year after all."

This time his wince had nothing to do with his injuries. "Tell me you're kidding, Sally. The last time I got stuck picking out a tree with her we were there for three hours and I nearly froze to death."

Sally grinned unrepentantly. "Dress warm. The temperature is plummeting and forecasters are predicting possible snow showers all week. I'll let Captain Walsh know he can come in and see you now. Catch you later."

Lucan leaned against the gurney like an old person, surprised at how difficult it was to do something as simple as pull on his pants. He had them halfway up his legs when Todd and the captain entered.

"Wow. You're a mess. Those bruises have to hurt. How's the head?" Todd greeted.

"Throbbing, and thank you so much. Did they get him, Captain?"

"No." Walsh eyed him with a dark look. "You could have been killed."

Lucan resisted an impulse to shrug. "He lost control around the corner. There was nowhere for me to go. The driver was Jordan Fillmont."

"You're sure?"

"I saw his face right before he rammed me."

"Okay, good to have confirmation. The car belonged to him, but the uniformed officer never got a look at his face. We couldn't be sure he was the driver. We recovered nearly forty thousand more in cash from the house."

Lucan whistled. Todd helped him into his shirt after watching him struggle. "Thanks. No wonder he was trying to get back inside. What about drugs?"

"No sign of any so far, but DEA is helping with the investigation." He ignored Lucan's sour expression. "There are other things to account for the money as you well know. Theft, blackmail…or it could be the guy simply didn't like banks. What did you get at Forest Oaks?"

Lucan related what he'd learned while he fumbled with the buttons on his shirt, feeling all thumbs. Todd made notes as he talked.

"Berringer will check out the groundskeeper tomorrow." The captain waved off the start of Lucan's protest. "You will take the next four days off. Doctor's orders. Besides, we don't have another unit available right now to give you."

Todd offered him a sympathetic look. "Your unit's so much scrap metal. They had to cut you free, in case you don't remember."

He remembered. At least most of it.

"Take it easy for the next few days," Walsh ordered. "I can't afford to lose anyone until we catch these killers targeting the wealthy."

"Another house got hit?"

"No, thank small mercies. Now rest."

"Thanks, Captain. Todd, will you see if you can find someone out there so I can sign a release and get out of here?"

As they left, he bent to retrieve his shoes. The room started to spin and go gray at the edges. Strong, supple fingers gripped him, keeping him from collapse.

"Easy there, hero. Let me get them."

Kyra's sexy contralto startled him. "What are you doing here?"

"At the moment, keeping you from falling on your face. Sit." She yanked a plastic chair over beside him. "I'll get your shoes."

"You aren't supposed to be driving around in your car."

"I'm not. You didn't say anything about me driving your mother's car. She sent me to check on you. I gather this sort of thing happens often?"

There was genuine concern in the warm blue depths of the eyes that regarded him.

"No. I can truthfully say this is the first time I've tried using my car as a Jersey barrier."

"From what Todd says, it leaves a lot to be desired."

And when had she and Todd come to be on a first-name basis? "What are you doing?" he demanded as she bent down and lifted his foot.

"Putting your shoes on for you."

"I'm perfectly capable of putting on my own shoes."

Kyra gave him the same look his mother used when he said something foolish. "You just demonstrated that you can't without falling flat on your face. Besides, turnabout is fair play. You took my boots off for me, so I put your shoes on for you."

A surge of physical awareness slammed into him. This wasn't supposed to happen. He was always cool and collected. Hadn't his ex-wife claimed that was part of his problem?

Cool and collected was the last thing he felt as Kyra deliberately caressed the arch of his foot before sliding his shoe on and tying it deftly.

"You're playing with fire," he warned.

"Really? I thought it was a shoestring."

He reached out, tangling his hands in her hair. Aches and pains were banished as desire arced between them.

"You're hurt," she reminded him, sounding breathless.

"Not that hurt." Her lips trembled under his, warm and achingly soft.

"Whoops."

Flynn's voice snapped the connection. Lucan straightened up to glare at his brother. "Your timing sucks."

"So I see. Hi, I'm Flynn O'Shay. You must be Kyra. My mother said you'd be here."

Red-faced, she hastily put the other shoe on his foot and tied it before looking up. "Nice to meet you. I was just helping Lucan get his shoes on."

His eyes twinkled. "Uh-huh. I do the same for my wife every morning. *She's* pregnant," he teased. "I'll have to try it your way tomorrow."

"What do you want?" Lucan growled. The biting edge of frustration made him grumpy. The simple kiss had left his body demanding more.

"I come bearing a gift offer. We picked up the new minivan. Whitney wants you to take her car for now. Your unit's toast and I know you never got around to replacing your old clunker. You may as well use her car. It's only taking up space in the garage until we can sell it. Besides, you've been drooling over that car ever since she let you drive it."

"Very funny."

"What sort of car is it?" Kyra asked.

Flynn's eyes lit up. "A Mercedes-Benz E 320 convertible with a six-cylinder engine, four-speed automatic and it's in mint condition despite the fact Whitney let this guy behind the wheel once."

"Why are you getting rid of it?"

"I'm a fireman. Whitney's about to have our first child. While it's a dream to drive, it just isn't practical. If you're interested, I'm sure Whitney would give you a good deal as well."

"Forget it," Lucan told him. "I'll call Whitney."

Flynn grinned smugly. "He's been lusting after that car, too."

"Too?"

Flynn gave her a meaningful look. Kyra's skin reddened, but she didn't look away. "It sounds like a great car."

Lucan came to his feet, annoyed for no good reason. "I'm going to find a nurse and go home."

"You're in luck," an older woman with a clipboard told him stepping into the overcrowded cubicle. "I'm a nurse."

KYRA DROVE LUCAN TO his home, still shaken as much by that simple kiss as the panic she'd felt when Maureen had told her Lucan had been hurt in the line of duty. Her first thought had been to rush to his side. She barely knew the man, yet somehow it felt as if she'd known him all her life.

She liked his family. At least the ones she'd met so far. They all had such big, loving hearts. Kyra felt at home with them in a way she hadn't since the death of her parents. She sneaked a look at Lucan and found him watching her.

Her pulse began racing. She could still feel the sensation of Lucan's lips on hers.

What had she been thinking? No matter how irresistible she found him, any sort of relationship with Lucan O'Shay was out of the question. She hadn't succeeded in getting the last man out of her life quite yet. She certainly wasn't ready to take on a long-distance relationship with a sexy, handsome cop.

"I did some checking," she blurted out in a rush. "I can't find a record of Jordan Fillmont until shortly before he met my sister."

Lucan straightened painfully, but his expression went all cop again. "What are you talking about?"

She told him what her search had yielded, and what it hadn't. "Obviously, I don't have access to everything, but Dowling has a pretty good research team and I asked for some help. There's no service record, no criminal record, no credit statements going back more than three years. In my line of work, that's a red flag."

"You involved Dowling people in a criminal investigation?"

His scowl pursed her lips. "It's what we do, Lucan. Don't look a gift horse in the mouth. Most of the research was my own. It's as though Jordan Fillmont didn't exist until two years ago."

"Did you tell Captain Walsh about this?"

"I didn't have a chance, but I'd think you'd be grateful for a little help. This creep married my sister and nearly killed you."

"This is a police investigation."

"Well pardon me, but Dowling works closely with police departments around the world. Instead of complaining, why don't you take the information and have your people run their own check?"

She could hear the rising anger in her voice and strove for control. "He'll have left fingerprints all over his car. Have them run the prints. I'm betting Jordan Fillmont is an alias. What do you want to bet it's a case of identity fraud? We need to find out who he really is."

Lucan started to say something she knew she wasn't going to like, but stopped before the words were uttered. Instead he opened his cell phone and pressed a button. His expression was still angry.

"Todd? Listen, have someone run Fillmont's prints. *Jordan Fillmont* may be an alias. No, just run him. Oh. You did? Okay. I am resting! Let me know when you hear something, all right?"

He hung up scowling. "They're running his prints. Todd will let me know what they find."

"Good."

"You need to let us do our job, Kyra."

"I'm not stopping you," she snapped back. "But my sister is missing and I intend to find her. Casey's just another case to your department. She's *my* sister."

He rubbed the side of his nose with a knuckle and the anger faded from his expression. "I know. We're going to find her. Turn here. My house is four doors down on your right."

Still fuming, she stared at the small, family-sized house

tucked between its brightly lit, lavishly decorated neighbors. His house looked dark and abandoned by comparison. Her anger faded as quickly as it had come. How long had he been coming home to an empty house like this?

She turned his mother's car into the driveway and put it in Park, leaving the engine running. "Are you sure you don't want me to go fill your prescription?"

"No. A couple of aspirins and I'll be fine."

"Tough guy, huh?"

"That's me. You want to come in?" he invited.

Excitement raced through her at the suggestion but common sense won out. "I can't."

"That's right. Your boyfriend is in town."

It was on the tip of her tongue to tell him Simon was no longer her boyfriend, but she held the words in check. "His plane was delayed. I told him I'd see him tomorrow."

"I shouldn't have kissed you."

She couldn't read his expression in the dark, but her heart pounded as if she was running a race. "No harm done." She barely managed to keep her voice steady under that fixed gaze.

"Maybe I should try again."

Her body quivered in ready agreement. "That wouldn't be wise." She couldn't believe she sounded so calm when her heart was racing so fast.

For long seconds he simply stared at her. She nearly told him then. She wanted nothing more than to go inside and learn where this crazy attraction might lead.

The moment shattered. He lowered his gaze. "Sorry. Do you know how to get back to my mom's from here?"

With a shaking hand she indicated the GPS system on the dashboard. "I can find it. Do you... Will you need any help?"

Say yes.

"No. I can get my shoes off without falling over. Don't worry." His tone was cool.

She barely stopped her hand from reaching out to him. "Sorry, Kyra. That was uncalled for. I'll be fine."

Her stomach was taut with emotion. "I'm glad."

He reached for the door handle. "Thanks for coming. And for driving me home."

"Get some rest, Lucan."

"'Night."

She winced as he stepped painfully from the car. A blast of frigid air swept inside. She shivered hard, and only partly from the cold. She watched his gingerly progress to his dark front porch, wondering if she'd just made a huge mistake.

He unlocked the front door and turned to wave before going inside. Kyra waited for a light to go on before she turned on the GPS system and typed in Maureen's address.

Swallowing hard, she put the car in gear and slowly pulled back onto the street.

BY THE FOLLOWING MORNING, Lucan was regretting his decision not to fill the prescription. There was no part of his body that didn't ache. He spent the morning fielding telephone calls from family and friends.

His mother insisted he come for dinner. Neil was bringing his family and she wanted to see for herself that he was all right. Whitney called and insisted she and Flynn would drop off her car that afternoon. Even Ronan called from Seattle, where he had a layover before flying home.

The only person he didn't hear from was Kyra. He shouldn't have kissed her. And he definitely shouldn't have compounded the situation by threatening to do it again—no matter how much he'd wanted to. He owed her another apology.

But he still wanted to kiss her again.

Todd's phone call gave him an unexpected jolt and a reason to talk to Kyra in person. As soon as Whitney and Flynn dropped off the sports car and left after marveling over the colorful side of his face, he pulled on his coat and gloves and headed out.

The clouds overhead were pregnant with the threat of snow, but at least the cold wind had died down. Lucan rehearsed what he wanted to say all the way to his mother's house only to find it empty. Stew bubbled in a pair of slow cookers and the scent of fresh-baked pies filled the air. He was about to help himself to a slice of apple pie when he heard cars pulling into the driveway.

An evergreen tree covered the top of his mother's car. His mother and the boisterous children spilled out once it came to a stop. Kyra stepped out next, followed by a tall, athletic-looking man. So this was the boyfriend.

The man immediately set about removing the tree from the top of the car even as Lucan's brother Neil and his family pulled up with a tree on top of their car as well. Lucan tamped down a left-out feeling as the happy group descended on the house, stirring noisy memories of times past. His mother greeted him first, then went in to check on the food, leaving him to face the rest.

"Hey, Lucan. Nice bruise," Neil said cheerfully.

"How come you aren't working?" he replied.

His brother cocked his head. "It's Friday. I took the day off. What's eating you?"

"Nothing. Hi, Phyllis." His sister-in-law carried the baby, but paused to kiss him on the cheek and eye the bruise near his temple.

"Sally didn't do it justice. Are you really okay?"

He kept his hand from reaching for the spot. "You know me. Hard-headed. Here. I'll get the door. Hey there, Sean, Duncan, Mary Kay. Did you pick out a good tree for your house?"

"Yep. Simon found us the perfect tree," Sean, the eldest announced.

Lucan eyed the muscular man heading for the door

carrying the large tree from his mother's car effortlessly. "Glad to hear it."

Kyra followed in his wake, her long leather duster cinched tightly at her waist, her face ruddy from the cold. She looked windblown and more desirable than ever.

Simon and the tree swept inside past him with a nod of thanks. Kyra paused, gazing up at him with worried eyes. "You look tired."

"What I am is freezing. Let's go inside. I need to talk to you."

But once they were inside her boyfriend strode over, thrusting out his hand. "You must be Lucan. I'm Simon Testier."

Lucan expected a bone-bruising grip as he took the extended hand, but Simon's handshake was merely firm. This was a guy who had nothing to prove to anyone. Grudgingly, Lucan decided he could like the man.

"Great family. It was nice of you to take such good care of Kyra." The *for me* went unsaid.

He held Simon's gaze. "Seems to me she can take pretty good care of herself."

"No question of that, right babe?"

Babe? He glanced at Kyra's annoyed expression.

"Don't call me babe."

Trouble in paradise? He shouldn't care, but it pleased him anyhow.

"I need to help Maureen get supper ready." She turned on her heel and walked away.

Simon immediately turned back to Lucan as if oblivious to her annoyance. "Neil tells me you play sports. Ever tried any of the extreme sports?"

"I'm a cop."

Simon chuckled. "Good point."

Lucan had been fully prepared to dislike Simon, but as Neil wandered over and joined them, Lucan began to see why Kyra would be taken with the man. Simon was cheerful, friendly, outgoing and knowledgeable in a number of areas besides sports. He knew how to draw people into a conversation. He was well-traveled with a good sense of humor and a ready smile. Lucan really wanted to dislike him, but found himself enjoying their conversation.

There was no opportunity to get Kyra alone in the crowd. They were getting up from dinner when his cell phone rang. Lucan excused himself and took the call on the front porch despite the bitter cold and lightly falling snowflakes. His mother's flashing white Christmas lights bathed the porch with soft illumination.

"How are you feeling?" Todd asked in his ear.

"Like I was run over by a truck."

"It was a sedan."

"Thanks so much. Did you get anything from the groundskeeper?"

"Yeah. His name is Carlos Ruiz. Ruiz left the country club because another job he applied for came through right after he started working for them. The new job pays more and the work is inside. His story checks out. He says he never met Fillmont and I believe him. I think he's a dead end."

"Too bad."

"Yeah, well, here's something to make you sit up. The first husband is missing as well."

"Bowman?"

"Yeah. NTS fired Milt Bowman six months ago for cause. He was drunk and got into a public brawl with a client. Bowman moved out of his apartment right after that and fell off the radar. I'm trying to get a lead on him now. This wasn't his first assault, either. He broke up a bar six months before that. It cost him a pretty penny, but he made restitution. He was on probation at the time of this last assault."

Lucan's mind spun with possibilities even as the front door opened and Kip came outside holding Lucan's coat.

"Aunt Kyra says if you're going to stand out here like a fool, you should put your coat on."

Todd laughed in his ear. "You're outside?"

"Yeah. Thanks, Kip." He took the coat gratefully as the boy scurried back inside. "Neil and his family are here. The noise level is a bit much."

"And you love it. What about Kyra's boyfriend?"

"He's here, too."

"And?"

"He's a nice guy. You'd like him."

"Too bad."

Wasn't it just? "She's part of a case, Berringer."

Todd chuckled. "Yeah, the most interesting part."

"I'm disconnecting now unless you've got something else."

"I already told you Kyra was right. Jordan Fillmont didn't exist until a bit under two years ago."

Lucan sucked in a breath. "So what about his prints?"

"We still have a computer hiccup. I'm told we should have an answer back by morning. I'll let you know."

"Call me."

"Sure thing. Stay warm."

Kyra stepped outside dressed in her butter-soft duster and matching gloves. Once again she wore those sexy knee-high boots that turned his mind in a direction it had no business going.

"Did Todd learn anything?" she asked.

With a shrug, he related what Todd had told him. From her pocket, Kyra pulled a long blue-green cashmere scarf that was instantly tossed by a gust of cold wind. He took a step closer as she struggled to wrap it around her neck.

"Let me."

"I can do it."

"I imagine there isn't much you can't do, but why not let me help?"

She stopped trying to brush her sassy brown hair away from her face with one hand and those gorgeous blue eyes widened in awareness. She released her grip on the scarf as he lifted the material away and wound the scarf around her neck.

"Cold?" He was standing too close, but when she didn't step back, neither did he.

"Yes." Her gaze softened. A gloved hand reached out to lightly touch his cheek.

"What are you doing, Kyra?"

"That bruise looks awful."

But her eyes were saying something else entirely. The twinkling Christmas lights revealed her heightened awareness.

"You're playing with fire. Your boyfriend's inside," he reminded her.

Regret flashed in her eyes. Her hand dropped from his face, but her chin lifted and she still didn't take a step back. He had only to bend the slightest bit to brush those soft lips once more. The reckless urge nearly won out, but he wasn't about to come between Kyra and Simon.

"I don't poach." Lucan stepped back leaving her to fuss with the scarf.

"I'm not a trophy."

"No, you aren't. But I hope Simon appreciates you."

Flustered, she looked away and managed to get the scarf settled to her satisfaction.

"I'm driving Simon back to his hotel," she told him.

"I'll do it. There may be slick spots on the side streets."

"I live in Boston, O'Shay. I know how to drive in winter weather."

The door opened on a blast of warm air and noise as Simon Testier stepped outside. He was dressed in his expensive coat and gloves. "All set, babe?"

"Yes. And stop calling me babe."

Simon didn't look the least bit abashed. "Nice meeting you, Lucan. You've got a great family there."

"Thank you. I appreciate your help on the big tree hunt."

"No problem. I haven't shopped for a tree since I was a little kid. It was fun. We'll catch you later." And he swept Kyra off the porch and down the steps to his mother's car.

Lucan didn't move until the car turned the corner. Too bad the guy wasn't a jerk. He really would have liked to hate Simon Testier.

Chapter Nine

"What happened to your car?" Simon asked Kyra as they climbed into Maureen's sedan.

"Nothing. It's in her garage and this one is parked right here so she told me to use it." Kyra didn't feel like explaining about the incident at the mall.

Simon chatted on, unaware Kyra was still shaken by those brief minutes alone with Lucan. Lucan had wanted her and she wanted him. The timing couldn't have been worse. Life wasn't fair.

"Hey, you asleep over there?" Simon asked.

Kyra managed a weak smile. "Just thinking."

"Must be deep thoughts, babe. I don't think you've heard a word I was saying."

"I've asked you not to call me that."

"It's a term of endearment. I can't help myself."

She glanced at his earnest features. He probably couldn't. Time to end this relationship once and for all and she'd figured out exactly how to do it. "I'm glad you came."

Simon settled back smugly.

"My sister is probably dead."

"Ah, babe, don't say that. There's always hope. Your detective seems to have a lot on the ball. I like him."

She gritted her teeth but managed a smile. "So do I. But

I have to plan for the worst. My apartment is too small for all of us. I was thinking we should probably find a house."

Simon stilled. "You love that apartment. *I* love that apartment."

"There isn't enough room in it for all of us," she reiterated, sensing his rising consternation. "But I'm sure we'll find something that will work."

"Wait. Us?"

"Yes. You, me and the children. I think we should have a quick wedding." She didn't dare look over at him for fear she'd laugh.

"You're planning to keep them?" Simon shifted in his seat.

"Of course I'm going to keep them. I'm their aunt, their only close relative." She felt his gaze boring into her and kept her eyes on the road. "There won't be time for a trip to Vegas, I'm afraid so it will have to be a justice of the peace."

"Uh, slow down there, Kyra."

"Don't worry," she assured him placidly. "I'll handle the details. We can go ring-shopping as soon as I get back to Boston."

"Kyra," he shifted some more. "You know how I feel about marriage."

"Of course, but we have the children to think about now. We have to do what's best for them."

"I don't think," he cleared his throat. "I don't think I'm the best role model for children."

"You'll be great," she assured him happily. "You'll have to give up some of your extreme sports, of course. That isn't an example I want to set for impressionable young minds, but we can work out the details later. Did I tell you how glad I am that you flew all the way here just to help me?"

"Kyra, I'm happy to *help* you, but I've never seen myself as father material. And a wedding… You're great, you know that. Smart, sexy and a lot of fun. But marriage and a family… Babe, I don't think I can go that route."

It was hard to conceal her elation as she sensed victory so close at hand. "I know this isn't what you wanted, but don't worry. You'll make a terrific father. You did great today."

"That was just…you know, temporary. Kyra, look, I like you. I really like you. But I told you up front I don't want the whole marriage-and-commitment thing."

"I know," she told him seriously. "But now I have the children to consider."

A tiny part of her felt guilty for using her sister's situation and the kids like this, but surely Casey would forgive her. The thought sobered her. Casey might not be around to forgive anything.

"I really am going to have to be their mother now, Simon."

Simon excelled at sports and his job. He knew exactly how to woo a woman and make her feel special. But at heart, Simon was a self-centered person with an inflated opinion of himself. If she could get him to break things off with her now, he wouldn't keep trying to get back together and they'd be able to work together without friction. And she was going to need a job with three children to raise.

"I get what you're saying, Kyra. But I need to sleep on this."

"Of course, but the sooner we make preparations, the easier it will be for the kids." And the grim part of her knew that was true. "I need to get the boys back in school and see about a nursery school for Maggie. She adores you already."

"She nearly threw up on me."

"You tossed her in the air right after she ate."

"See? That's what I mean. I don't know anything about little kids. I'm not cut out for fatherhood. Uh, the hotel's right there up ahead. You can drop me off in front."

"Don't you want me to come up so we can discuss this?"

"Not tonight, babe. I'm bushed. All that fresh air today really tired me out. I'll sleep on it and call you in the morning."

He leaned over and gave her a quick, light peck.

"Okay, Simon. I have a lot of planning to do anyhow. Sleep well."

"Yeah, you, too."

He was out of the car and moving away. Moving out of her life for good unless Kyra missed her guess. She steered the car back into traffic as a light snow began to fall. There was a sense of relief, but also a trace of sadness. Simon was a good guy. He just wasn't *her* guy. They'd had a lot of fun together, but something had always been missing.

Like the excited quiver of anticipation that thoughts of Lucan stirred in her.

She had to stop thinking about Lucan. This was a physical attraction that was doomed before it went anywhere at all. She was drawn to him. What heterosexual woman wouldn't be? But Lucan could be every bit as irritating as Simon when he turned his cop on.

Still, even his cop half had a softer side that was highly compelling. He'd held her and offered comfort as a friend. He'd been there for her when she'd needed him. And there was no getting around their growing attraction. It wasn't one-sided by any means. But was it merely sexual interest on his part?

Lucan was one of those rare alpha males without the inflated ego. That alone held her attention. But he lived and worked here in Maryland. Her life was in Boston.

Wasn't it?

On impulse, she detoured to drive slowly past his cozy little house. Dark and silent, it looked so sad and neglected amid its neighbors' brightly shining Christmas lights. The house reminded her of the one her parents had owned when she was young.

Lucan had been married before. Had his wife picked it out? Why had they divorced?

The windshield wipers swished aside the snowflakes

splattering against the glass. The streets were becoming slick as the temperatures continued to fall. She needed to get back to Maureen's before the roads turned really slippery. Still, as long as she was this close…she turned onto her sister's street and stopped across from Casey's house.

Kyra didn't want to believe Casey was dead. She clung to the hope that Casey would return for her children. They would be so lost without her. *She* would be lost without her sister. Casey had always been there. Kyra had taken that fact for granted.

"Where are you Casey? Your children need you. *I* need you."

Her eyes burned with unshed tears. She quickly blinked them back. If only she'd kept in closer touch with her sister. Maybe then she'd know what was going on here.

No matter how this turned out, Kyra silently vowed to change her busy lifestyle. The constant travel was wearing thin anyhow. It was time for a change. A lawyer with her background should have no trouble finding another job. She even had a few contacts here in the D.C. area.

Being around Maureen had made her realize how much she missed being part of a family. Kyra had friends, but when it came right down to it, she had no real roots in Boston. Okay, she loved her cozy apartment, but she traveled so much she was rarely there to enjoy it.

If the worst had happened and Casey was dead, there was no reason Kyra couldn't move here. It didn't really matter where she lived. Family was what mattered.

Kyra closed her eyes. She couldn't bear to think of Casey lying dead in a shallow grave somewhere. She wanted her sister to appear right now and explain. Together they could handle Jordan and Milt and anything else that came along.

As she opened her eyes a blurred motion in the rearview mirror sent thoughts scattering. Fear leaped into her throat. A dark-clad figure pelted out from behind the car.

Kyra gaped at the muffled figure. The person yanked at the locked passenger door and raised an object in his hand. Even as her mind recognized it as a gun, he turned it, smashing the butt forcefully against the window. Two hard blows and the glass gave way.

Belatedly, Kyra threw the car in gear and hit the gas. The heavy sedan lurched forward. Tires spun frantically as they sought traction.

She barely avoided a parked car as the sedan slid before righting itself. Only dimly did she register the masculine voice ordering her to stop. The gun in his hand fired.

He was trying to kill her!

She cornered too fast at the intersection, ignoring the stop sign, and nearly lost control. Panic sent her head swiveling back over her shoulder as she corrected. *Two* men chased after her. Flame flashed from both weapons. They really were trying to kill *her!*

Then she was around the corner driving as fast as she dared on the worsening streets. Panic filled her. She couldn't think of anything beyond getting away.

In minutes she was lost on the slick side streets of the sleepy subdivision. Where was she? How did she get back to the main street? She needed lights and people so she could call for help.

Someone was actually trying to kill her!

Snow began changing to sleet. The droplets pinged off the windshield. Icy wind rushed in through the broken window. Kyra shook with cold and shock. How did she get out of here? Were they following her?

Why? Why was someone trying to kill her?

Frantically trying to stem her panic, she turned onto street after street, more confused than ever. She was lost! What was she going to do? There was no sign of pursuit, but that didn't mean they weren't back there somewhere.

And abruptly she recognized the string of townhouses.

She turned down the street and left the housing development. A busy convenience store sat on the corner. Kyra pulled in, snagged a newly vacated parking spot and turned off the engine.

She was shaking all over. Sleet pummeled the car with increasing fury. Despite her gloves, her fingers felt numb. She struggled to find the cell phone in her purse by feel. Pulling it out, it took her three tries to flip it open.

She panicked as a new car pulled in the lot. Her breath caught in her throat. Petrified, she watched, unable to move until a woman climbed out and hurried inside.

The sound of her rapid breathing filled the car. She had to calm down. She was too isolated sitting here all alone. The men hadn't followed her. They couldn't know where she was. But she couldn't just sit here in Maureen's car with the shattered window. Kyra grabbed her purse and dashed inside.

A blast of heat slapped her in the face. Piped-in Christmas carols sang cheery words to the line of people in front of the register. Kyra ran over and shoved aside a man about to set his parcels on the counter.

"Please, I need help. It's an emergency!"

The customer she'd elbowed gaped in horror. "You!"

She stared at him blankly before his features registered. "Mr. Garber?"

The assistant manager from the movie theater took several steps back, nearly tripping over the person behind him.

"Are you following me?" he demanded.

"Don't be stupid." Kyra turned back to the clerk. "There are two men with guns chasing me. We need to call the police!"

The cashier promptly moved from behind the counter.

"Again?" Garber demanded in disbelief.

"Yes! One of them tried to get in my car. He broke out a window and shot at me when I drove away."

Garber plopped his bag of dog treats and the six pack of soda on the counter.

"What is it with you, lady?"

The clerk locked the front door. "Everyone should go to the back of the store," he told the half dozen or so people riveted by the scene. "I will call the police."

One man had already pulled out a cell phone. Kyra heard him ask for police assistance and was reassured. Two people fled, but reluctantly, most of the customers allowed themselves to be herded to the back of the store. Kyra went with them, ignoring the commotion. She opened her own cell phone once more and immediately found a connection. Thankfully, she'd thought to program in Maureen's phone number. To her profound relief, Lucan answered on the third ring.

"Lucan! Two men tried to get in the car while I was stopped. They broke out the passenger window and shot at me when I drove away."

"Where are you?" His voice was calm but hard.

"In a convenience store near your house. The manager locked the front door and someone called the police."

"Okay, go to the rear of the store and keep down. Stay away from the windows. Have Salman or Ranji or whoever is working there tonight make sure the back door is bolted. I'm on my way."

"You are not hurt?" the clerk asked as she closed her cell phone.

"No. No, I'm fine. Thank you. Detective O'Shay said you should check that the back door is bolted."

"He is a smart man. I will do this."

The man who had called the police looked more annoyed than nervous. "Damn carjackers. No one's safe anymore."

Kyra didn't respond. If only it had been something as simple as a carjacking attempt, but that was too large a coincidence.

"Personally, I think you're a police groupie," Mr. Garber stated loudly. His expression was sour. "I don't think anyone was after you at all. You probably broke out your own window just to get attention."

Kyra ignored him. She was still shaking and despite the warmth of the store she shivered. Her mind raced. She'd believed the man at the mall had been after Kip. But what if he'd been after her?

Why?

A plump, middle-aged woman tapped her on the shoulder. "Mrs. Fillmont? Are you okay? You're shaking."

Kyra stared at the woman.

"I'm Robby's mother, Nancy Riblenowski. We live a couple of doors down from you. Kip and Robby go to school together."

"Fillmont? That's not the name she gave the police this afternoon," Garber announced loudly.

Kyra ignored him. "I'm sorry. I'm not Casey," she told her. "I'm her sister, Kyra Wolfstead."

"Oh." The woman looked confused. "We've never met. That is, your sister and I have never met. They just moved in a short time ago and I'm ashamed to admit I haven't gone over and introduced myself to her. We've just waved in passing, but I was sure... You look a lot like her."

"Yes, I do."

And it hit her. Excitement electrified her. It made perfect sense when you considered how similar she looked to Casey. Casey was older, of course, but those men must have thought she was Casey! They weren't after her or Kip, they wanted her sister! That meant Casey was alive!

"Does the carjacking have something to do with all the commotion at your...at your sister's house the other night?"

Kyra stared at the woman, barely registering her question. Casey had to be alive!

"I know the police were looking for Kip that night, and

the news the next day said your sister was missing," the woman continued.

Every eye was on her. Garber's mouth was gaping in astonishment, but she continued to ignore him and tried to focus on the friendly neighbor. She banked her excitement, bursting to tell Lucan her suspicions.

"I really can't talk about that right now," she managed.

"Oh. Well if there is anything I can do…"

"Thank you. That's very kind of you."

Casey was *alive!* She had to be alive. It was the only thing that made any sense. Relief made Kyra giddy. She must have swayed because suddenly the man with the cell phone was reaching for her.

"Are you all right, lady?"

"Fine. I'm fine." If Casey was alive she was better than fine. Kyra prayed Lucan would hurry.

Her euphoria died almost as quickly as it had come. Casey loved her kids. She'd never leave them alone like this unless she had no choice. So for some reason, Casey couldn't come home. They had to step up the search to find her sister.

Flashing blue and red lights announced the arrival of the police, but it was Lucan O'Shay whom Kyra waited for.

LUCAN'S RELIEF AT SEEING Kyra was out of proportion to what he should have felt for someone he barely knew. He'd passed his mother's car, seen the broken window and nodded to the officer examining what appeared to be bullet holes in the trunk and side of the car.

Her call had sent terror right through him. He'd nearly killed himself on the slippery roads, driving as fast as he'd dared to get here. It was crazy. She was part of a case. She lived in Boston. She already had a boyfriend.

And her features lit the moment she saw him. He pulled her into his arms and hugged her tightly, ignoring the people and fellow officers milling around.

"You're okay?"

"I'm fine. Casey's alive!"

He released her and stepped back. "What?"

Excitement radiated from her as she explained. Lucan scowled, trying to decide how to temper her enthusiasm without crushing her hope. But once again he'd misjudged her. She wasn't blind to reality.

"I know I could be wrong, Lucan. But it fits! Why would that man have tried to grab me at the mall yesterday? Or the men try to get into my car? They think I'm Casey. That means Casey is alive!"

"Or they think she is," he added softly.

Lips pursed, blue eyes darkened, but she nodded. "Yes. And I have to believe she is. I think she sent the kids to the safe room and then got away from the men who came to her house. I think she's hiding, afraid to come home. Maybe she thinks Jordan has the kids."

He covered her sleeve with his hand. "I'm not saying you're wrong."

"We have to look harder for her. Maybe get out a message that the kids are safe with me and she should go to the police. She's probably afraid of her husband."

"Which one?"

She stared at him blankly.

"Both men are missing, Kyra. And we know Fillmont tried to get back into the house once already."

"He was looking for the money."

"Maybe. We don't know for sure what he was after. What if the money belonged to Bowman and she hid it from him? We don't know what's going on here or who that money belongs to."

Her brow creased. "You're right."

As she fell silent, Lucan glanced around. He nodded to Ranji and noticed a familiar face glaring at Kyra. "Isn't that—?"

"Mr. Garber from the movie theater," Kyra agreed. "He was in line when I came in." She wiggled her fingers at him and Garber turned quickly away. "I don't think he likes me very much."

"What's he doing here?"

"He was buying dog treats and soda when I came in. He must live nearby."

"Okay." He could see the exhaustion setting in on her features. It had been a stressful day for both of them. "Let me talk to the officers and Ranji and I'll get you out of here. The weather's turning nasty."

That proved to be an understatement. Sleet mingled with the snow that continued to fall. Even the truck that came to tow his mother's car had problems in the icy parking lot. Lucan eyed the situation in growing concern. Whitney's little sports car wasn't built to handle weather like this. The road crews were doing what they could, but if sleet continued to stream from the sky they'd never make it to his mother's. And by the time he got Kyra away he knew he'd been right. They weren't going to make it back to his mother's house.

Kyra sat tense and silent beside him as they crept along and the temperature continued dropping.

"Lucan?"

He didn't dare glance her way. Holding the road took his full concentration.

"Isn't your house closer than your mom's? Maybe we should go there. One wreck a week is enough for anyone. Let's not tempt fate more than we have already. It isn't even safe to walk out here."

"I noticed. I have a small house," he cautioned, "but I do have a spare bedroom." And he was trying not to think about her sleeping there under his roof. "Just make sure your boyfriend understands the situation."

"Simon isn't my boyfriend."

"Significant other?"

"Not even."

"He flew in from Germany to be here for you."

"No, he came because he can't accept no for an answer."

Had the other man proposed tonight?

"What was the question?" He barely managed to keep his tone light.

She sat silent for so long he was sure she wasn't going to answer. Then she sighed. "Simon's a nice person."

His stomach plunged. "I noticed."

"He's also vain, egotistical and controlling with a deep-rooted fear of commitment."

Lucan nearly looked at her then. "You wanted commitment?"

"Not with him. Remember, vain? Egotistical? Controlling? I like Simon. We work well together. He can be a lot of fun and we've enjoyed a personal relationship. But when I told him I didn't want to continue, he couldn't believe me. I don't think anyone's ever dumped him before."

"You *dumped* him?" He brought his attention back to the road just in time to keep from sliding into the curb.

"Keep your eyes on the road, please. That was close."

"Yeah. This car's too light."

"Maybe we should get out and carry it."

Lucan grinned. He loved her sense of humor.

"To get back to your question, I tried to extricate myself from our relationship," she continued. "That only made Simon work harder to reestablish one."

"You know that doesn't make sense, right?"

"Of course I know it. Talk to Simon. So tonight I gave him an opening and a reason to dump *me*."

Lucan tensed. She'd told Simon he'd come on to her?

"Your ego isn't too shabby either, is it? You weren't the reason."

She sounded amused which made him wince.

"*Fatherhood* and *commitment* are two words that make any happy bachelor quail."

He caught her drift, then. "He doesn't want you to take the kids."

"Nope. And I only feel marginally guilty for using this situation to my advantage. If Simon believes he's the one doing the dumping, it will make our working relationship run a whole lot smoother."

"You have a dark side, don't you?"

He sensed her smile. "I do whatever it takes to get the job done."

"You're a scary lady." His lips curved.

"I can see you shaking from here."

"That's tension. I'm keeping this expensive sports car from sliding all over the road by sheer force of will."

"Whatever works."

They fell silent while Lucan concentrated on creeping the short distance to his house. He was relieved to finally pull in his driveway and slide to a stop only partially on the grass. He sat there after turning the engine off to let his body unclench.

"Well, that was fun. Are you okay?" Kyra asked.

"Sure. As soon as I can summon enough energy to move we'll skate to the porch."

"I forgot my ice skates."

"I don't think you're going to need them." He rolled his shoulders trying to ease the pain of cramped muscles.

"I give a mean backrub. Let's go inside and see if I can unknot some of those tight muscles."

His head swiveled in her direction. "Not a good idea."

"Why not?" She flushed. "Oh. I'm not sure if I should be flattered or annoyed."

"Definitely flattered. I've seen you annoyed."

A smile flicked across her lips.

"I'll tell you what, Lucan, if you keep that sexy mouth of

yours to yourself, there won't be any problem we can't handle."

She opened the car door, allowing a blast of arctic air inside. He was pretty sure it wasn't cold enough to do the job.

Chapter Ten

Despite her bold words, Kyra was nervous when Lucan held the door open and she stepped inside his house. A surge of welcome warmth enveloped her. He hit a switch by the door and two floor lamps softly illuminated the cozy space.

Kyra was immediately certain that no ex-wife had decorated this house. Two large, unmatched but comfortable-looking recliners in shades of sand were paired with a worn but serviceable brown couch that had seen better days. Mismatched end tables and a scuffed coffee table perched on a forest-green rug. The overall effect was a cozy, inviting room where a man could kick back and relax.

No pictures adorned the walls, but family photographs dotted the shelves of an oversized bookcase that had been built over a real wood-burning fireplace. The shelves spanned the length of the longest wall. What should have been a mantel was a long shelf housing a ridiculously large television set. Games, game consoles and DVDs were neatly organized amid a wide array of books.

The room was orderly and if there was dust on the end tables, it didn't matter. This was an inviting, lived-in space that would be nice to come home to at the end of a busy day. It suited Lucan.

"Here, let me take your coat."

Kyra handed him the long leather duster. "I'd better take my boots off, too. I don't want to track water all over your hardwood floors." They were real hardwood and gleamed brightly even in the soft light.

"Need some help?"

His eyes twinkled. Another flush stole up her cheeks. If he noticed, she hoped he'd put her high color down to the cold. "What would you do if I said yes?"

"Kneel at your feet and peel them off one leg at a time."

Her stomach went into freefall. He was deliberately being suggestive, and her blush deepened. She couldn't remember when a man had affected her this way.

"I always do like to have a man at my feet," she retorted.

"Ah, well there is one small problem." A grin lurked at the corners of his lips. "I have to warn you that once I get down on the floor, I may not be able to stand again without help."

A laugh burbled past her lips. Lucan turned his grin free.

"Forget it, O'Shay. Nine-one-one is too busy for that sort of phone call tonight. I'll take off my own boots." And still smiling, she bent down to do just that.

"Have it your way then."

A gust of wind rattled the house. She heard the icy pellets striking the windows and suppressed a shudder. The storm didn't seem to be letting up at all.

"I think tonight calls for hot chocolate," Lucan continued. "I might have a bottle of red wine if you'd prefer. And I know I still have some of my mom's brownies in the freezer. Make yourself comfortable. I'll call her and let her know about the change of plans."

"I'm sure she's worried," Kyra agreed. "But why don't I call her while you go upstairs and get in a hot shower? I can manage two cups of hot chocolate."

Lucan hesitated.

"You can barely move," she pointed out. "That was an

intense drive home and you were just in a car wreck yesterday. A shower will relax your muscles and I'll see if I can work some of the knots loose when you come down. Go. And if you can find an oversized T-shirt or something I could borrow to sleep in that would be great."

"Are you sure?"

"Positive. I'm not helpless, Lucan."

"No." He smiled appreciatively, making her insides lurch. "You certainly aren't. Okay. Help yourself to whatever you need or can find." And he headed for the stairs, moving stiffly.

Kyra dug out her cell phone and called Maureen. The call was answered on the first ring. The older woman must have been sitting next to her phone worrying.

"We're fine, Maureen. We're at Lucan's."

"Then stay there, the pair of you," she ordered before Kyra could say more. "This is no night to be driving, especially in that car of Whitney's."

"I agree."

"Lucan said you had a problem?" she asked.

"You could say that. I'm fine, but I hope your car insurance covers bullet holes and a smashed passenger window." Kyra explained quickly.

"Don't you be worrying about that car. It's just glad I am that you weren't hurt," Maureen told her. "The children and I will do fine until this weather improves. The tots are abed. I'm headed there m'self. You and Lucan get some rest and we'll talk in the mornin'."

Kyra smiled. It had been a long time since she'd had a mother worrying over her. The feeling was surprisingly nice. "Thanks, Maureen. If there are any problems with the children, give me a call."

Hanging up, she made her way to the kitchen. Like the rest of the house, the room was small, cozy and orderly. Maureen had taught Lucan well. No dirty dishes lurked in the sink and while he didn't keep a fully stocked refrigerator, he was probably seldom home to do much cooking. All the basics were there including eggs, juice and cheese. The freezer held bread and carefully labeled leftovers. They were in no danger of starvation.

She pulled out the package marked Brownies and set it to thaw on the counter while she searched the small pantry for the hot chocolate mix. Water ran in the pipes overhead. She tried not to picture Lucan naked in the shower.

Giving him a massage was probably a bad idea. While Lucan tried to keep things impersonal, she'd seen the darkening of his gaze, felt the quickening of his breath, tasted those firm lips. He might be hesitant to get involved, but he was a sexy, virile man. Of course he'd be willing.

Was she?

Yes. Which was nuts. Did she really want to complicate the relationship between her and the one man who was actively trying to help her find Casey?

Selfishly, she did want that, but Kyra had never been a slave to her emotions and she wasn't going to start now. Later, after Casey was home and safe, maybe then they could see where this attraction led. They were both intelligent, consenting adults.

The house shuddered under a stiff blast of wintry air. Sleet had iced over the windows. The lights flickered, went out for a breathless instant and came back on again. The house might be cozy, but it would cool fast if they lost power.

Kyra set aside the hot chocolate mix, turned off the pan of water she'd set to boil and went looking for a flashlight. It didn't surprise her that Lucan was prepared. A large, heavy flashlight sat under the sink. She carried it into the living room, where logs and kindling were already neatly laid in the fireplace. Once she opened the flue it didn't take her long to get a crackling fire started.

Satisfied when it caught, her attention was drawn to the contents of the bookcase. Because he was a cop, she expected Lucan to go in for mysteries and crime dramas. And there were some of those along with mainstream thrillers, but there was also science fiction, fantasy, biographies, even some old Westerns. She was pleased to find several of her own favorite authors and a couple of movies she really liked.

The photographs sprinkled about gave insight into his family and friends. Kyra found it easy to pick out Lucan's siblings. The brothers had similar features even though each of them was very individual. His nieces and nephews also shared that common look that made them unquestionably part of the clan. An old photo of Maureen and her husband showed a striking couple. No wonder their sons were so handsome.

Kyra lifted a small bird carving beside the photograph. The piece was amazingly detailed and obviously handcrafted. She wondered where Lucan had come across it. Several other small wood carvings were sprinkled about. Lucan obviously collected them.

Hearing him moving about overhead, she returned to the kitchen and set the water to boiling. Putting the brownies on a plate, she zapped them in the microwave for a minute before taking them and some napkins into the living room. Minutes later she returned with two steaming cups of hot chocolate as Lucan was descending the stairs.

A jolt of sensual awareness shattered her calm. No one should look that good dressed in black sweatpants and a plain black sweatshirt. He carried himself with an air of confident authority like some sleek, dangerous panther. The man should come with a warning label.

And when she saw that he'd taken the time to shave again, a heavy sensual heat swept her.

Thankfully, he didn't seem to notice her loss of composure. Those intelligent eyes smiled as he took in the fire and accepted the hot cup from her hand.

"Good thinking," he told her with a nod toward the fire.

Warmth started somewhere low in her belly at the sound of his voice. She was grateful when hers came out sounding normal. "I was afraid the power might go off permanently. It's still sleeting and snowing outside. Please tell me that isn't all the wood you have and that the rest of the logs aren't out in the yard."

He smiled. He had a killer smile.

"No. I have a covered carrier on the back porch with enough wood to keep us warm well into the morning."

Relaxed, he was irresistible. Kyra tried to tamp down the erotic image his words had conjured, out of all proportion to what he'd actually said. She couldn't seem to shake the want building inside her. What was wrong with her? She was vividly aware of him on a purely sensual level. This was so not like her.

As if sensing her confusion, he regarded her, his head tipped slightly to one side. Gray eyes darkened to a deep charcoal as their gazes locked. The atmosphere of the room was charged with new tension.

"Kyra?"

The power flickered and went out. She drew in a long breath and released it slowly. Only the hard masculine planes of his face showed in the flickering firelight, darkly mysterious and intently focused on her. Before she could speak over the pounding of her heart, the lights came back on, only to flicker several more times.

"I think that's my cue to bring in some more wood."

His voice was thick with awareness. Or was that her subconscious willing it to be so?

She set her mug beside his on the end table between the two recliners. "I'll give you a hand."

He didn't protest and she was thankful that he didn't touch her, either. If he had, she was certain she'd have lost any vestige of control. She followed him to the screened-in back porch, grateful for the icy chill of the wind-driven sleet. They were both shivering by the time they collected enough logs and kindling from under the tarp to last them several hours.

An aberration, that's what it was. Proximity and the situation were playing with her mind. Of course she found him attractive. What heterosexual woman wouldn't? But she could handle the situation.

If only he hadn't shaved.

By the time they'd washed their hands and returned to the living room, the hot chocolate had cooled to the perfect temperature for drinking. Kyra took the nearest recliner. With a knowing lift to the corners of his lips Lucan took the other, leaving a table between them.

He swallowed and smiled appreciatively. There was nothing sensual or inviting in that smile. It was as if he'd turned off the attraction with a switch. But he couldn't do anything about his wicked good looks, and they were keeping the edge of her physical awareness keen.

He picked up a brownie and strong white teeth closed over it. He chewed as if relishing the taste and swallowed. Kyra picked up her hot chocolate and swallowed hastily.

"I put fresh towels in the bathroom upstairs," he told her conversationally. "I also left you a clean pair of sweat pants, a T-shirt and a sweatshirt. The ice is building up out there so I think it's a good possibility that we might lose the electricity for several hours at some point. Even with the fire going, the house will cool off."

She bit into a brownie, concentrating on savoring the rich, chocolate taste only to find him watching her intently. She nearly choked. It was not her imagination. Lucan was attracted but he was going to let her set the pace.

"I'm going to bring a blanket down and spend the night on the recliner in front of the fireplace."

His voice was low, soft, compelling. She could drown in that sound.

"I've slept on it more than once."

Easy to picture him, tired after a long shift, falling asleep in one of the chairs with no one around to wake him and send him to bed. Firelight flickered over his features.

"How long have you been divorced?"

He stared at the fire but didn't appear discomfited by her nosy question.

"Five—no, six years now. Bess didn't understand what being a police officer's wife entailed. I was in uniform back then and she hated shift work, especially when it included weekends and holidays. Six months into the marriage we both realized the sex was good but the relationship wasn't going to work. Bess needed a husband who worked a nine-to-five job and I was never going to be that person." He shrugged. "The divorce was amicable. I even went to her next wedding."

He flashed her a smile.

"She married a friend of mine. He works for the county. He's home every night at six and they're blissfully happy. They have a two-year-old and another child on the way."

"Does it bother you?"

"Not at all. I introduced them. It was a little awkward at first, but we've gotten over it. Bess and Ray are nice people. You'd like them."

Hearing her own words for Simon tossed back at her, she returned his smile.

"You might want to take a shower yourself before we lose power," he continued, lifting his shoulders to relieve tight muscles.

"I will, but if you'd like me to rub some of the knots from your neck and shoulders I should probably do that now while the muscles are still mostly relaxed from your shower."

Her heart hammered at the way his eyes blazed.

"I think," he told her softly, "we'd better skip the massage."

He was right. She knew he was, but she couldn't seem to stop the words tumbling past her lips. "Afraid, O'Shay? I really do know what I'm doing. I dated a fitness trainer a few years ago. He taught me how to give a massage. Not to brag, but he claimed I was a natural."

His gaze seemed to smolder. He stood slowly, filling the space with the sheer masculinity of his form. "If you're trying to suggest another way of keeping warm, just say so, Kyra. O'Shays don't do subtle, as my sisters-in-law will tell you."

Heat flamed her cheeks. She rocketed to her feet, facing him. "I was offering to massage your neck and shoulders, not take you to bed. When I want sex I'll ask for it."

"Then ask me."

The low, soft-spoken words stole all the air from her lungs. Somehow he'd bridged the distance between them, standing so close she could see a small nick on his jaw where he'd cut himself shaving.

For her.

Her heart beat like a wild thing. He ran a knuckle down her cheek.

"What are you doing?" she gasped.

"Preparing to kiss you."

"You have to prepare?"

His low chuckle sent waves of passion flowing through her blood.

"To do it right."

His hand closed around her back. He drew her in slowly, giving her time to change her mind.

As if.

He crushed her against the hardness of his body and

took possession of her mouth. There was such need in that kiss that it overwhelmed her. It was like drowning. Like being reborn. She didn't want it ever to stop.

She was moaning deep in her throat as she mashed herself against him trying to get closer. She ran her hands over his back, tangling her fingers in the softness of his still-damp hair. She could feel the hard thrust of him as their bodies sought a closeness barred by clothing.

And when finally he lifted his head, she wanted to cry. "Easy. Easy, Kyra. We have all night."

She stared at him, bewildered, feeling the tension in him, knowing he wanted her as much as she wanted him.

He pulled her head gently against his shoulder, stroking her hair, then cupping the back of her head. "I don't want to hurt you and I'm losing control."

His voice was rough, thick with need. She smiled against his sweatshirt and lifted her face. "You won't hurt me. You would never hurt me."

His response was lost as he reclaimed her mouth.

A LONG TIME LATER she sat curled beside him on the deep couch, loving the play of the dancing flames against his bare skin. Her fingers absently traced the scar from a bullet wound he told her had nearly killed him. She'd kissed that scar and others when they'd made love more slowly the second time.

"I'm glad you weren't killed."

"You just came close," he told her with a satisfied rumble. "I'm too old to be this horny."

"Poor old man. What was I thinking?"

"You were able to think?"

She laughed at his teasing and stood. "You never did get that massage."

"Really? Because I'm feeling pretty boneless at the moment."

With a laugh she began gathering her clothing from the tangle spread around them. The air hadn't felt cold before, but she could feel the chill now despite the fact they still had power and heat.

"You're beautiful, you know."

Color rushed to her cheeks. "I'm not." Embarrassed, she tossed him his sweatshirt. "Put something on before we both freeze."

He held the shirt while his dark eyes watched her intently.

"If you don't stop looking at me like that, I'm coming back over there." Was the man inexhaustible?

"Mentally, I'd like that a whole lot. Physically, I'm not sure I can move, but I'm willing to try again if you are."

"Forget it, O'Shay. I'd die of embarrassment trying to explain to your mother how I killed you." His throaty laugh made her heart sing. "I'm going up to get that shower now."

Knowing he was still watching, she added an exaggerated sway to her walk as she crossed to the stairs. He reached her before she'd mounted two steps. For such a large man, he could move with speed and silence when he wanted to.

She whirled, and he handed her the flashlight. "You might need this."

"Thanks."

SHE HAD PLENTY OF time to consider the ramifications of what she'd just done as she let the shower spray wash over her. There wasn't an ounce of regret in her. But fear? Oh, my yes, she was scared. Deep down where it really mattered scared. Because no matter how much she told herself they were consenting adults and it had been an enjoyable way to spend a long cold evening, she knew the truth.

Almost from the moment they'd met, she'd been drawn to the strength of him, the kindness in him. That first time had been sex, pure and simple. But the second time…the second time had been something else entirely. She could love this man. The deep, for-evermore sort of love she'd read about but never thought to experience firsthand. Nothing had ever felt this right.

Could her timing be any worse?

She left the shower and took her time getting dressed. Halfway down the stairs she heard his cell phone ring.

"O'Shay," he answered.

She would never tire of the sound of his voice.

"Todd? What are you still doing on the clock at this hour? Don't tell me our thieves struck again."

She rounded the landing to see him standing in front of the fire with his back to her. He was dressed down to his shoes and she realized he'd gone out back for more wood.

He tensed visibly and swore. "Where? You're sure? Since *when?* Why did it take so long…?"

Kyra froze on the final step gripping the heavy flashlight tightly. Her heart suddenly fluttered like something gone mad. Some indefinable quality in his voice sent tendrils of fear shooting through her.

"How bad? And you're sure it's Casey?" He swore again. "Okay. I'll tell Kyra."

Her other hand gripped the banister for support. Casey couldn't be dead. She just couldn't be.

He moved to stand in profile, scowling and listening intently.

"No. Yeah, it can wait until morning. Who've you got…? Right. Thanks, Todd. I'll talk to you later. Yeah. You, too."

His expression was forbidding as he closed the phone and abruptly spotted her standing there.

"You heard?"

She couldn't even manage a nod. She stood frozen, waiting for the words she dreaded to hear.

"They found your sister."

Chapter Eleven

Kyra's stricken features sent him rushing to her side as he realized what she must be thinking. "God, I'm sorry! Casey's alive, Kyra."

"Alive?"

He supported her as she swayed. Strong, powerful, there for her.

"She's in the hospital. She's going to be fine."

It was too much. She let him guide her to the chair.

"Sit down."

"I thought…I mean, you said…" she shook her head. "I don't know what you said. She's really alive?"

"Really. She was in a car accident. Apparently she took an off ramp too fast. The car plunged over the embankment into a thicket of bushes and trees, trapping her in the car. They found her yesterday morning, after she worked her way out and managed to crawl to the top of the embankment. An alert officer noticed recent damage to the top of the guardrail and spotted something red. He stopped to check it out."

Kyra felt weak. "She always liked bright red."

"Good thing. Her red coat stood out. She was unconscious and badly battered when she was found. Several broken ribs, a broken arm, sprained ankle, assorted cuts and bruises and I'm not sure what else, but all in all she was exceptionally lucky."

Kyra closed her eyes and forced her lungs to release the breath they were holding. "Thank God. We have to go to her." She started to get up and he pressed her firmly back down.

"Not tonight."

Anger flared. "Of course, tonight! If you won't take me I'll go by myself."

"Kyra, she's been unconscious for much of the time since they found her yesterday. Casey isn't going anywhere tonight and neither are we. We'd never make it. You know that. And even if we did, you wouldn't be allowed to see her at this hour and disturb the other patients. We'll go in the morning as soon as the roads clear."

She muttered softly. "You're right. I know you're right. But…"

"She's your sister. I understand. I'd feel the same way if it was one of my brothers." And nothing, not even an ice storm, would keep him from finding a way to the hospital.

He was trying to think of a way to get her there when without warning, the lights winked out. This time they stayed out. The snapping hiss and crackle of the fire filled the sudden stillness.

"I think that's it for the electricity tonight," Lucan told her.

Kyra nodded, studying his expression. "There's more, isn't there? What aren't you telling me?"

Surprised by her perception, Lucan hesitated. "I'll tell you as much as I know. Do you want something to drink first? I have beer and wine or the stove is gas. We could make—"

"Lucan, I'm okay. Casey's alive. It's the miracle I've been praying for. But if they found her yesterday morning, why didn't someone call to tell us until now?"

Lucan perched on the edge of the couch watching the firelight play across her features. "She was unconscious and she didn't have any identification."

"Her picture's been on the news."

"She's banged up, Kyra. At first they thought her jaw was broken. It isn't," he hastened to add, "but she was in a lot of pain."

Kyra winced. "What else?"

"She was driving a stolen car. They traced the license plate and coincidentally, the car belonged to a woman about Casey's age. Since Casey had no identification and none was found at the scene, they assumed she was the owner."

Kyra nodded acceptance even though her tension was palpable. "And?"

Lucan sighed. "And there was an empty beer can in the back of the car. That led them to think she might have been drunk when she went off the road. They knew she had to be traveling at a high rate of speed to go airborne and clear the guardrail the way she did."

"I see where this is going."

He nodded. "They thought she was a drunk driver. And they thought they knew who she was."

"Okay, I guess I see that."

"When they learned the car was stolen—"

"They thought Casey stole the car." Her frustration rose.

"The officer should have identified her sooner, but he didn't. When someone finally did, he started questioning her about the money."

Kyra was furious. "And Casey told him she didn't know what he was talking about and he treated her like a criminal."

Lucan nodded unhappily. "Todd was finally called in tonight. Casey was upset—"

"I can't imagine why," she snarled.

"—and frantic about her kids. Todd assured her that you had them and they were safe."

Kyra began to pace. "Why didn't she call me?"

"Does she know your cell phone number?"

"Of course she…" Kyra stopped. Consternation sent her head shaking from side to side. "Probably not. Who knows phone numbers any more? She'd have it programmed into her cell phone."

"Which is in her purse at her house," Lucan agreed. "She's scared, Kyra."

"Can you blame her? Talk about police brutality. She's a victim here, not a criminal!"

"I know. We'll go to the hospital first thing in the morning and get this straightened out, I promise. The important thing is she's safe and she's going to be fine."

Reluctantly, Kyra nodded, but she was still upset. "I was right. That's why those men were trying to kill me. They thought I was Casey. They don't want her to testify against them." And her eyes went wide. "She's in danger, Lucan. They're going to try to kill her!"

"Todd thought of that. She was moved to a private room. There's an officer stationed outside her door. We're not completely incompetent."

Kyra barely acknowledged that. Her mind was spinning.

Lucan spoke quietly. "They must have been watching the house. They probably saw you leave with Kip the other day and followed you thinking you were Casey."

"I bet they want the money."

"Possibly. It's a reasonable assumption."

Anger pinched her features. "I'm going to kill Jordan when we find him."

His smile held no humor. "Let me arrest him. He's not worth a murder charge."

"It was a figure of speech…more or less."

His lips curved. "I know."

"She's really going to be all right?"

"I wouldn't lie to you about that, Kyra. Casey's going to be fine. And we should try and get some rest. Tomorrow is shaping up to be a long day. Do you want to spend the rest of the night down here with the fire or go upstairs? It's going to get pretty cold in here, but I have a lot of extra blankets."

"I won't sleep now."

"You won't do Casey any good if you don't at least try to rest. We're both tired. If you don't want to lie down, I'll get some blankets and we can sit down here by the fire, okay?"

"Yes. I'd rather do that."

Lucan took the flashlight and headed upstairs. But listening to the fury of the storm still lashing the house, he wondered if he'd be able to get her to the hospital come morning.

MORNING BROUGHT AN END to the storm, but not the expected warm-up. Ice clung to the branches of trees and bushes and coated the roads and sidewalks. Every available surface outside glistened despite the fact that the day was gray and heavily overcast. It would be midday at least before the side streets or sidewalks would be navigable.

Kyra had fallen asleep against his shoulder, nestled in her blanket. She looked deceptively soft and fragile. Lucan didn't want to disturb her, but biology insisted he get up. Every muscle in his body protested as he slipped free and stood.

He debated adding logs and kindling to the fire. Only a single smoldering log was left, but he decided to wait for fear of waking her. He headed upstairs to use the bathroom.

The bruise on his face had darkened and diffused a bit more. And once he stripped he noticed several others he hadn't realized he had. He wanted a shower, but he didn't want to use all the hot water, so he settled for washing up at the sink.

A chill had settled over the house, as expected. He dressed in a warm shirt and pullover sweater. Finding another sweatshirt and polo shirt for Kyra to use, he left them in the bathroom and went back downstairs. She stirred, opening her eyes when he checked on her.

"Morning," he greeted. Her tousled hair and eyes cloudy with the remnants of sleep lent her a vulnerable air. He kissed her forehead, wishing he could offer her a cup of hot coffee to start the day. He would have liked one himself, but he didn't have any instant.

"Hmmm." She stretched her face up for his kiss. "You taste minty. What time is it?" Her voice sounded scratchy with disuse.

"Almost eight-thirty."

That widened her eyes to full alertness and brought her bouncing up off the couch. "It can't be! I never sleep this late!"

"Relax. We aren't going anywhere for a while. The roads are impassible." He held up the battery-powered radio he'd taken from his bedroom. "I had this on upstairs. Traffic lights are out all over town. They're asking people to stay inside while road crews treat the streets. There are accidents everywhere. The hospitals are filled with people who've fallen and broken bones. We can't even get to the car until some of the ice starts to melt."

She scowled, taking in his words and looking around the room. "The electricity is still off."

"Yep. All over the area. They're saying it could be some time before we get it back."

"That bruise on your face looks painful."

He smiled. "I seem to have a few new ones."

Kyra blushed, but tilted her head up for his kiss.

"Hmm. You taste good, but I need to use the bathroom."

Relieved that there was none of that awkwardness that often comes the morning after, he smiled. "I left you some clean clothes, but remember the only hot water we have is what's still in the tank right now, so if you shower, keep it brief unless you favor cold showers."

She grimaced and paused to pull his head down for another quick kiss before hurrying up the stairs. Lucan watched her go before he sauntered to the kitchen to see what he could pull together for breakfast. He was humming as he pulled eggs and cheese from the refrigerator. He could get used to waking up to someone like Kyra every morning.

His cell phone rang before he could process that startling thought.

"Do you have power?" Todd asked in his ear.

"No. What about you?"

"None when I left. I'm at the hospital right now."

"Don't tell me you fell."

"Hey! I carry bags of ice melt with me everywhere in this kind of weather. No, Casey Fillmont disappeared this morning."

Lucan inhaled as the words crashed over him. "What happened?"

"As near as we can tell she walked out sometime after she was moved to that private room."

"There was supposed to be someone stationed there to protect her."

"He was called away."

Lucan cursed. "You're telling me she walked out in the middle of an ice storm? With a broken arm and fractured ribs?"

"And a bum knee and ankle," Todd added. "Yeah, I know, but that's how it looks."

"I don't believe it. Are you sure she walked out under her own power? What do the security tapes show?"

"The hospital was running on emergency generators at the time. There are no security tapes."

Lucan rubbed the back of his neck. Tension had returned with a vengeance.

"We've searched the area. She was too banged up to have gone anywhere on foot, but there's no sign of her."

"She didn't leave willingly." Lucan felt sick.

"There's no sign of a struggle," Todd insisted. "Her coat

and clothes are gone but there's no way to tell if she left because she was forced or because she wanted to leave. Manacuzzi was pretty rough on her. Thanks to him, she doesn't trust us. You can't blame her."

Lucan stared at the egg carton while his thoughts raced. After refusing to take her to the hospital last night, he did not want to tell Kyra that Casey had vanished. She would think the worst.

He thought the worst. He swore out loud.

"Yeah. I know," Todd agreed. "I got her description on the air right away. Do you want the media to carry the story? It will be a sidebar given the weather, but someone might have seen something."

"If they have her, she'll be dead before we find her again." He pictured Todd nodding agreement into the silence.

"Let's hold the good thought," his friend offered. "Let's assume she was ticked off and called a friend to come get her."

"In an ice storm." He could almost see Todd shrug.

"It's possible."

But not probable. "Any chance you could arrange a car for me to use?" Lucan asked.

"Walsh ordered you to take time off. You're supposed to stay home."

"Berringer…"

"The captain would have my head."

"Not if he doesn't find out."

"Yeah, right. Like that will happen."

"Ask Jessup to delay the paperwork a few days. She likes you. You can sweet-talk her into loaning me something from the motor pool."

"Walsh said there was nothing available."

Lucan waited in silence.

"Why don't *you* call her?" Todd demanded.

"She'll tell *me* no."

"Walsh will have my hide."

"Which one of us do you fear most?"

His friend swore. "Okay. But you're going to owe me big for this."

"You still owe me two," he reminded Todd.

"Petty, Lucan. Really petty. I'll see what I can do. But if Jessup says no…"

"She won't say no to you. Offer to take her to dinner in exchange. You know you've been wanting an excuse to ask her out. Here it is."

"That's it, partner. I'm taking you off my Christmas list."

"How will I ever survive?"

Todd hesitated. "You really think she'd go out with me?"

"I think she's been waiting for you to ask her out for the past four months. Stop being a wimp."

"She intimidates me."

Lucan shook his head. "You're a detective. Nothing intimidates you."

"Except a five-foot blonde who not only knows what a carburetor is, but can take it apart and put it back together again so fast it makes me dizzy. You know I'm not mechanical."

"Buy a book. Just get me a car that weighs more than a miniature terrier."

"I'm going to regret this."

Lucan's lips lifted.

"We don't have a thing in common," Todd complained.

"That's the fun part." Lucan disconnected and spotted Kyra standing in the hall. How much of the conversation had she heard?

She should have looked ridiculous dressed in his old high-school sweatshirt. The sleeves were rolled halfway up her arms and the hem hung well below her shapely hips. But Kyra looked as cool and in control as usual. And somehow she managed to be sexy in his old clothes and those sexy boots of hers. And she didn't look angry.

Yet.

Todd thought he was intimidated?

"Was that Todd?" she asked.

He wasn't ready to have this conversation. He turned back to the eggs and began taking them from the carton even though he was no longer the least bit hungry. "Yeah, I'll tell you about it after we eat."

"Tell me now." The light tone left her voice.

She seemed to have radar where he was concerned. "Todd's arranging for a cruiser so we can get out of here. He has a thing for the woman in charge of the motor pool."

Kyra came around to the side of him and laid her hand over his. "There's something you aren't telling me."

Her hand was so small and graceful against his big, rough, scarred one. "What are you, clairvoyant? I'm a cop. I'm supposed to be inscrutable and intimidating."

"And I've been a lawyer and an investigator almost as long as you've been a cop. In case you haven't noticed, cops don't intimidate me. Not even broad-shouldered tough guys like you. And I know when someone's prevaricating."

"I haven't lied to you."

"You're right, you're stalling."

Her hand fell away. Reluctantly, he turned to face her. "Casey went missing early this morning. She either walked out of the hospital on her own or someone helped her. Either way she's vanished."

For a moment, shock left her speechless. Kyra gaped as if trying to absorb the words. "I thought there was an officer stationed outside her room."

He repeated what Todd had told him.

Her face pinched with fear. "Jordan has her! Or those men!"

He shook his head. "We don't know that. It's entirely possible she walked out on her own."

"You don't believe that."

"I *choose* to believe that."

"If she did, she went home," Kyra announced with certainty. "She has to be crazy with worry over the kids. We have to get over there!"

"Not in Whitney's car." On that, he wasn't going to budge. "No car's safe on ice, but that one doesn't weigh enough to do anything but slide all over creation. We'll wait for Todd to bring us a cruiser."

"We can walk! She only lives a block away!"

"Ice skate, maybe. Walk?" He shook his head. "No way, Kyra. If you haven't looked outside, the world is one big ice rink at the moment."

"I can make it."

"I wouldn't bet against you, but if you fall and break your neck how is that going to help Casey or the kids?"

"Lucan, I have to go!"

He took her shoulders, holding her gently. "I understand. I do!"

She calmed slowly.

"Think about it. If Casey goes to the house, what's the first thing she's going to do? She's going to look for her purse and her cell phone and call you, right?" He watched her consider his words.

"We left them there." Her eyes were dark with worry.

He nodded and pressed home his advantage. "Wait for Todd."

"She could be in trouble by then."

"She could be in trouble right now. You know that, Kyra. I'm not going to lie to you." He squeezed her shoulders reassuringly and released her. "As soon as the sun comes out the ice will start to melt. This is D.C., not Boston. We heat up fast around here."

"So I noticed."

Her feeble attempt at a joke surprised him. At the same time, it reassured him. She'd accepted what he'd said. "Regrets?"

"None."

He kissed her forehead. "Put some water on to boil while I start these eggs."

"I'm not hungry."

"Neither am I, but we need to eat something. This could be a long day."

Kyra nodded once and turned to find a pan. Her shoulders were stiff, telling him she was still upset, but she was smart and logical. They both knew the odds were high that Casey wasn't going to call. And there wasn't a thing they could do about it at the moment.

They worked together and sat down at the table. Kyra ate dutifully in silence for several minutes before setting down her fork.

"We need to find out why Jordan Fillmont has no history. Why haven't they run his prints yet?"

Lucan paused, a fork halfway to his mouth. "There was a computer glitch."

"That was yesterday. They must have something by now."

He chewed and swallowed without tasting. He set his fork down as well. The entreaty in her eyes was more than he could stand. "You're right. Todd may have heard something. We'll ask as soon as he gets here."

They cleaned the kitchen and Kyra helped him fold the blankets and take them back upstairs. Todd still wasn't there so Lucan tried using a snow shovel on the iced-over front porch.

"No ice melt?" Kyra asked after nearly falling.

"Sure. Two full bags in the trunk of my unit."

"Not helpful, O'Shay."

"Tell me about it."

The sun made a belated appearance between the clouds and the temperature began to rise. Kyra went back inside to call Lucan's mother and check on the kids. When she returned a short time later he could see she was upset.

"Maggie woke with a bad dream last night. Your mom had a hard time getting her calmed down. She lost some bauble her bear was wearing and she's having ten fits over it. Even Kip is upset. I talked to him for a minute and he kept saying he had to find the bear's necklace or Maggie wouldn't stop crying."

Lucan heard her guilt that she wasn't there to deal with the children.

"Mom's got years of experience. She'll calm them down. There's nothing we can do right now."

"I know. I'm just frustrated."

He held her tight. The sound of an approaching sand truck raised his head. To Lucan's surprise, Lieutenant Chrissy Jessup was right behind the truck in an unmarked cruiser. Todd's unit followed close on her bumper.

Chrissy had clout. The county truck dumped an extra load in front of his house and into the apron of his driveway so she and Todd had a place to park. The sun had stopped playing around and was finally contributing wholeheartedly to the de-icing process. The sound of dripping water was everywhere.

Todd got out first and began spreading ice melt in their path so they could walk up the driveway without falling.

"Lieutenant," Lucan greeted the woman.

"Nice parking job, detective." Jessup inclined her head toward Whitney's car. "You should treat that better. That's one sweet piece of machinery. Berringer says your sister-in-law is selling it?"

"Yeah. I'm going to take it off her hands," he heard himself say. Glancing at the small car, he realized he really did want to own it, no matter that it was out of his price range and totally impractical. He'd always coveted that car.

"Lucky man. Mind bringing it by one day so I can look it over?"

"I'd appreciate it, actually."

She gave him a piercing stare. "That hurts to look at."

Self-consciously, he fingered the swelling on the side of his face.

"I haven't seen what's left of your unit yet, but I hear you had to be pried loose."

He shrugged. "I left my can opener at home that day."

With a lopsided grin, she winked at Kyra. "I'm Chrissy Jessup."

Kyra took the proffered hand. "Kyra Wolfstead. Nice to meet you."

Todd finished spreading the ice melt around and joined them.

"Did we get results back on Fillmont's prints yet?" Lucan asked.

"I don't know. I didn't make it as far as my desk this morning."

"Don't hold your breath," Chrissy told them. "Rhea left early yesterday and didn't make it in this morning. Rhea Loosh is in charge of that department," she added for Kyra's benefit. "Her kid fell on the ice. She had to take him for X-rays. We were supposed to have lunch today so she called me to cancel. And while I hate to rush off, I need to get back." The last was aimed at Todd. To Lucan she added, "Try not to wreck this unit, okay? I just got it running again."

"Do my best."

Todd rolled his eyes, but he had a silly grin on his face as he handed Lucan a set of keys and followed in Chrissy's wake.

"Interesting lady," Kyra commented.

"She comes from a long line of auto mechanics, including her mother. Add to that four older brothers and I'd have to say Chrissy knows more about cars than anyone else I know."

"Todd seems smitten."

Lucan locked the front door. Together they made their

way to the parked cruiser, careful to stay in the areas Todd had salted. "The two of them have been dancing around each other for months. He says she intimidates him."

"I can see why. Should make for an interesting relationship. I like her."

"So do I." He glanced at her. "I'll take you to my mom's."

"After we stop by Casey's house."

He frowned.

"Don't say no," she admonished.

Lucan sighed. "I'm willing to drive past and see if there's any sign that someone went inside." He hesitated, not wanting to say it, but knowing he had no choice. "But I've been thinking about this, Kyra. You need to consider the possibility that Casey may not be an innocent victim."

Chapter Twelve

Kyra's chest tightened. "Casey's not a criminal. You're wrong."

"I hope so. I really do, but don't discount it out of hand. I know she's your sister, but you should prepare for the possibility."

Her cell phone rang before she could argue further. She answered as they climbed in the car.

"Hey, babe."

Kyra groaned, wishing she had checked the caller number before answering. "Simon, this isn't a good time."

"Has something happened?"

Kyra stopped herself from blurting out that the police had located Casey and lost her again. That she had spent the night in Lucan's arms and was very much afraid she'd fallen in love with the man. That her world was spinning out of control and she was feeling overwhelmed. "No."

"Okay, look, I thought over what you said last night. Kyra, I'm just not ready for fatherhood or the marriage thing. I like you. But we agreed from the start that this was no chains, no regrets, right? You can do better than me, babe. I'm a free spirit, a live-in-the-moment kind of guy. You ought to look for someone like O'Shay. He seems more like the hearth-and-family type to me."

Kyra closed her eyes against a sudden need to laugh hysterically.

"Anyhow, I'm heading back to Boston as soon as they open the airport again and I can get a flight out." He paused and added, "Unless there's something you think I can do to help you find your sister."

She glanced at Lucan. He gave no sign that he was listening even though she was certain that he was. The car's wheels spun, searching for traction as he pulled away from the curb.

"There's nothing you can do right now, Simon. But thanks for the offer." She appreciated that he meant it, but wished he'd hurry and disconnect.

"So we're okay then? Friends?"

"Of course."

"Good. That's good. Let me know when you find Casey. If there's anything I can do to help you with research or whatever give me a call, okay?"

"Absolutely," she agreed absently as Lucan turned onto Casey's street. "I have to go now, Simon. Have a safe trip back." She disconnected.

"Simon's heading back to Boston," she told Lucan.

He pulled in front of her sister's house and put the car in Park before looking at her. "Are you all right?"

"I'm relieved." She held his gaze.

"Should we talk about last night?"

Her lips curved. "What, you want me to tell you how good you were?"

Twin spots of color bloomed on his cheeks but he never lost a beat. "Praise is always welcome."

Kyra laughed softly. "Egotist."

He smiled and turned his attention to the house. Ice reflected diamond-bright and glittery beneath the morning sun. Nothing marred the brilliant perfection of the surface sweeping the lawn from curb to porch.

"There's no sign anyone has been here."

Her disappointment was crushing.

"Where would she go, Kyra?"

Lucan's gentle tone made her want to cry in frustration. "I don't know."

"She must have friends, someone she would call."

"I don't know her friends." The admission was painful. She hadn't realized how very little she actually knew her sister.

"Wait," she implored as the car started to roll forward. "Aren't we going to check inside?"

"If she made it this far we'd see footprints or tire tracks in the driveway. Something." Lucan waved a hand to indicate the yard.

She stared at the pristine expanse defeated. "I was so sure she'd come here."

Putting the car back in Park, Lucan turned to her. "Most of the side roads are still a mess. No one with any sense is out here driving around, Kyra. Let's assume she got a ride from the hospital and is hunkered down somewhere waiting until she can get here safely."

Kyra released a sigh. "You're a good man, Lucan O'Shay."

"Glad you think so. I'll take you to Mom's now."

She stayed the hand that would have put the car back in gear. "What are you going to do?"

"Swing by the precinct and see if someone in Rhea's office has the results of the fingerprint check on Fillmont."

"You're supposed to be on leave."

His lips curved ruefully. "It will only take a minute."

"I'd like to go with you."

He hesitated. "What about the kids?"

Kyra wavered. She should go straight there, but the kids were safe for the moment and she had to know. "You said it would only take a minute."

Lucan hesitated, then nodded. "Okay. It's on the way."

"Thanks." She leaned over and kissed his cheek. When she would have pulled back, Lucan stopped her, kissing her with gentle thoroughness before letting her go and putting the car in gear.

"You have a way of sending my common sense right out the window."

"You're a good man, O'Shay."

"You said that before." He shot her a glance. "But you should know I'm not *that* good."

She smiled. "You were pretty extraordinary last night."

"Tell me that again when I'm not driving on ice."

"Where would be the challenge in that?"

Lucan grinned. He knew she was determined to stay cheerful and upbeat even though she was worried sick over Casey.

The ice continued melting as the sun raised the outside temperature. Between the melting and the sand the county trucks had laid down, they made it to the station without mishap.

Once inside the busy precinct, Lucan was hailed by fellow officers. He waved and returned greetings, but kept walking, Kyra at his side.

"Is your captain going to be upset you came in?"

"Probably."

He led her to an open room housing computer work stations. A handsome black man looked up as they approached his desk. "O'Shay! Nice color you got there," he greeted, staring curiously at Kyra.

"Thanks." Lucan didn't bother with introductions. "Anton, do you know if a match came through on Jordan Fillmont?"

"Sure did. About an hour ago. I left the info for Berringer. I was told you were taking time off to recover." He looked pointedly at Kyra once more.

"I'd introduce you, but it's better if I don't. What you don't know can't get me in more trouble."

The man called Anton raised his eyebrows and shrugged. "Your funeral, man."

Anton opened a different file on his computer. "Jordan

Fillmont, aka Ronnie White, with a history going back to sealed juvie records. They caught him in a fencing sting in Illinois two years ago. He turned state's evidence against a major player with some nasty connections. A conviction would have been his third strike. He knew he was going down hard if he didn't cooperate, so he helped them nail a guy they wanted for a string of homicides. Then he fell off the radar."

"Witness protection?" Lucan asked.

Anton's teeth flashed once more. "Got it in one. Ronnie White became Jordan Fillmont. Now it looks like he's our problem."

"What was his M.O.?"

"B and E. Breaking and entering," he added for Kyra's benefit.

She smiled. "I'm a lawyer."

"Oh." His eyebrows went up another notch.

"Forget she said that," Lucan advised.

"Right." He returned his focus to Lucan.

"Would you print me out a copy of the report?" Lucan asked.

"Uhhh... How much trouble am I going to get into?"

"None if you don't mention it to anyone."

"Uh-huh. It's gonna cost you. I need a bear carving like you did for Rhea. My wife really liked that bear and she's got a birthday coming up right after the holidays."

Lucan glanced at Kyra and quickly looked away. "How about a cat?" he temporized. "I've got one almost finished."

"Even better! Sometimes I think she likes that big lazy tom of hers more than me."

"Who wouldn't? Cats are neat." Lucan inclined his head at the messy desk.

"Low blow, O'Shay. Just remember who's doing who a favor here."

"When's her birthday?"

"The twelfth."

"I'll try to have it finished by then."

"Deal." He handed Lucan a printout of the report.

Kyra didn't say anything until they were outside the building and heading for the car. "I would have waited in the car if I'd known my presence was going to get you in trouble."

"Don't worry about it."

"Okay. So those woodcarvings on your bookshelves are your work?"

He tensed. "No. My grandfather did those."

"And the bear and the cat?"

He shrugged without looking at her. "I whittle a little. My grandfather was better. Rhea did me a favor once, so I gave her a bear for her birthday."

She said nothing more until he got in the car and started the engine. Lucan was embarrassed, she realized. The tips of his ears were red and not from the cold. He avoided her gaze.

"I thought whittling was a lost art. Did your grandfather teach you how?"

"Yes. It's just a hobby, Kyra."

Whittling explained the small scars on his hands and fingers she'd noticed earlier when they'd made love, but obviously his hobby was something he was self-conscious about.

"I've always wanted to learn how to use a scroll saw, myself."

His eyebrows rose in surprise. "A scroll saw?"

She shrugged. "I love some of the fancy scroll work I've seen in Europe. I'd love to be able to do that myself."

"Why don't you?"

"No time, no place to set it up, and I wouldn't know where or how to begin." Now it was her turn to be embarrassed so she changed the subject. "I've been thinking. I don't see Jordan giving up his life of crime just because he was given a new identity."

He shot her a hard look. "Reading my mind now?"

"Common sense. You said you're having a crime wave involving thefts. We both know Jordan didn't make all that money Kip found in tips at the golf course."

"Ever think of trying your hand at police work?"

"My job is similar to yours in a number of ways." But she couldn't keep the pleasure from her voice. "So where do we go from here?"

He held her gaze. "You go to my mother's. I'm going to touch base with Todd and find out how many of our burglary victims belonged to the Oak Forest Country Club."

LUCAN DIDN'T COME INSIDE with her, but he promised to call and check in later. She half expected the house to be in turmoil, but the boys were playing a video game and Maggie was in the kitchen at the table drawing pictures with Bear perched on the chair at her side. Maureen bustled about preparing lunch and a pot of spaghetti sauce for later. Kyra didn't know anyone who made their own spaghetti sauce.

If Maureen's house had lost power it wasn't evident now. The aroma of baking chocolate filled the warm air. There were several types of cookies filling tins and cooling on racks on the counter.

"What can I do to help?" Kyra asked.

"Not a thing, lass. It's all under control. The wee ones are going to help me decorate the cookies later. The power came back on a short while ago."

"Did you find the missing necklace?"

"Aye. A great gaudy piece of glass it is, too. Young Kip was nearly as distraught as Maggie until he found it under her bed. The lad has a strong sense of responsibility. The house has been peaceable ever since it went back around the bear's neck."

Kyra pulled off her coat and gloves before squatting down beside Maggie's chair. "Hi sweetie. What are you doing?"

"Drawing a picture of Bear and Kip."

"And a very nice picture it is, too."

"You look funny."

Kyra followed Maggie's gaze to the rolled-up sleeves of the oversized sweatshirt and had to agree. "I do, don't I? Would you and Bear like to come upstairs and help me change into something else?"

"Okay."

"I'll be right back, Maureen."

"Take your time, lass."

The little girl was mostly silent, sitting on the bed watching wide-eyed as Kyra changed clothes. Not until she unrolled her jewelry bag did Maggie show any emotion. Her gaze fastened on a glittery necklace of dichroic fused glass in vivid shades of blues and violets.

"Would you like to wear this?" Kyra offered.

"No, Bear can wear it!" She opened the bear's vest to reveal a flash of color. Kyra saw what had to be Maureen's 'great gaudy piece of glass' and her heart stilled in her chest. It wasn't glass.

Heart now pounding rapidly, she reached out to touch the pendant. "May I see this, Maggie?"

The child nodded, still looking at Kyra's collection of jewelry. Kyra had handled many pieces of antique jewelry over the years in her job. While by no means an expert, she knew real gemstones when she saw them. Unless she missed her guess, she was looking at the brightest, largest, square-cut emerald she had ever seen in her life. The stone was set in platinum and framed by what could only be diamonds cut in a unique style. The pendant dangled from a piece of string.

"I'll tell you what." Kyra tried to keep her voice even and

nonchalant. "I'll trade you this necklace and my pearls for that one." The pearls weren't real, but the choker went with a number of her outfits and she wore it frequently.

Maggie hesitated.

"How about if I give you these, too?" She held up a pair of crystal earrings that tossed small rainbows around the room. "We can put them thru Bear's vest like this." And she pushed the posts through the material, capping them with the backs.

The sparkle of the glass and the offer of four for one was enough to convince the child. "Okay."

Kyra tried to contain her excitement. Maggie removed the necklace and accepted the other two in its place. Kyra helped her wrap the much-too-large necklaces several times around the bear's fake fur. Maggie was thrilled. She ran off to show her brothers.

Kyra carried the pendant into the bathroom where the light was stronger. Definitely platinum, diamonds and an emerald big enough to choke a horse. This was heirloom jewelry beyond a doubt. She didn't need a jeweler's loupe to know the stone and setting were real. She could practically feel the age of the piece. But where had it come from?

Kip suddenly appeared in the doorway, his face a mask of fear. "Give me that! It's Maggie's!"

"It's okay, Kip. We traded."

"No! You can't keep that!"

She stilled. "Why not, Kip?"

The boy looked away, trembling in his agitation.

"Where did Maggie get it, Kip?"

He wouldn't answer. His expression of guilt was enough.

"You found it where you found the money, didn't you?"

The boy studied his shoes.

"Kip, look at me. It's okay. I told you. I'm your aunt and your lawyer. You aren't going to get into trouble."

Disbelief was written across his features. "I had to give it to her! Maggie wouldn't stop crying. Mom said we had to be quiet. When I tied the string on it and gave it to Bear she stopped crying."

The thought of what he'd gone through made her ill. She gentled her voice, wanting to touch him, but afraid he'd withdraw. "It's okay, Kip. Really. You found this with the money?"

He nodded.

"Was there anything else?"

He looked back down. "A ring," he mumbled. "Green like that."

Excitement zinged along her nerve endings. "What happened to the ring?"

"Brian put it in his pocket. When he went to the bathroom it fell out and rolled down the broken vent on the floor. I couldn't get it out."

Kyra tried not to let her voice show any emotion. "This was at your house?"

He nodded.

"Detective O'Shay will get the ring. Did you find anything else with the ring and the pendant and the money?"

He shook his head.

"Okay. These belong to someone, Kip. Maggie can't keep this. But she may keep what I gave her. I wish you had told me."

"I thought you'd be mad that we lost the ring."

She hugged his stiff body soothingly. "I'm not mad, Kip. Honest I'm not."

The child did not look appeased. "Jordan will be."

Her heart was suddenly pounding once more. "Why will Jordan be mad?"

"'Cause they're his. He put them in a sock with some money when he came home late."

"How do you know that?"

"I saw him," he mumbled to his feet. "I heard Mom yelling at him. They woke me up. I was scared."

Afraid Jordan was going to hit his mother like his father had done, she realized.

"When it got real quiet I snuck out of bed to see if Mom was all right. Jordan was standing by the dresser holding them up and smiling. I thought he was going to give them to Mom like Dad used to do after they had a fight. Only Jordan put them in a sock with some money."

A direct link from Jordan to the stash they'd found. "Did he see you, Kip?"

The boy shook his head. Lucan would flip, but Kyra strove for outward calm. "This is important. Did you see Jordan put the money or the jewelry where you found it?"

"No. When I went to show Brian, the jewelry was gone." There was hope in his expression as he studied her face. "You aren't mad?"

"No, honey. You didn't do anything wrong at all." She wanted to ask if Jordan had hit Casey, but decided against it. "Your mother didn't know about the jewelry?"

He shook his head.

"Do you remember when this happened?"

"Uh, last Tuesday. I remember because I had a math test and I didn't do so good. Mom let me stay up late with her. She was mad because Jordan didn't come home from work that night. She was crying, but she didn't want me to know."

No eight-year-old should have to grow up like this. Kyra could have throttled her sister. "Will you tell Detective O'Shay about this when he comes over, Kip?"

"He won't arrest me for taking the jewelry or losing the ring?"

"Not a chance. I'm a very good lawyer."

Kip smiled, but it faltered quickly. "Do you think he'll ever find Mom?"

This time Kyra pulled him into a tight hug. "I know he will. And soon," she promised.

"Good," he mumbled against her shirt. "I want to go home."

"I thought you liked it here."

"It's okay, but I want my mom."

She squeezed him tenderly, trying not to cry. "I want her, too, Kip." The boy tightened his arms around her waist, returning the hug. "She's going to be so proud of you."

He pulled back and eyed her seriously. "Is she gone because of Jordan? Did he hit her like Dad used to when he came home late?"

"I don't think so, but I don't know, honey. I'm pretty sure if Jordan did hurt her, she's going to be okay."

He nodded solemnly.

Maureen called up the stairs to tell them lunch was ready.

"Go wash up and tell Mrs. O'Shay I'll be right down, okay?"

"Okay."

Kyra tried to call Lucan, but there was no answer. She slipped the pendant in her pocket, then thought better of it. Taking one of her gold chains, she attached it and fastened it around her neck as she headed for the stairs. Whatever happened, she didn't want to be responsible for something this valuable going missing again.

THE PEOPLE HE'D spoken with who had been robbed, had been members of the Oak Forest Country Club. That included the late Shereen Nestler and her husband. Lucan hung up after talking to Todd and drove away from the Nestler estate. Shereen Nestler should have been in New York with her husband the night she came home and surprised someone rifling her house. She'd changed her plans at the last minute, deciding to stay behind to attend a fundraiser for one of her charity groups instead. The plan had been to catch up with her husband the following day.

Lucan was revved. Todd agreed that this looked like a major break in the case. Even the captain was only mildly annoyed that Lucan hadn't obeyed orders. There was too much pressure to find the person or people responsible for the burglaries.

But if Casey Fillmont was involved in the woman's murder as well, Kyra was going to take it hard. And Lucan didn't want to think about how badly Kip would react. Sometimes, he hated his job.

Lucan drove back to his neighborhood thoughtfully. The streets were clear now except for the melted water everywhere. The roads would be a mess again tonight when everything refroze. This close to Christmas, that would mean big problems for late-night shoppers.

He parked in the street in front of Casey's house and walked up the driveway. There was no outward sign that she had returned, but like Kyra, he was betting she'd show up here eventually.

He was nearly to the porch when he saw movement inside. Lucan reached for his gun and radioed for backup. Whoever was in the house had seen him. There wasn't time to wait. He ran onto the porch, unsurprised to find the front door unlocked.

Standing to one side, he pushed it open. "Police officer!"

Footsteps pounded toward the back of the house. Lucan set off in pursuit. He rounded the corner of the dining room. Milt Bowman was just reaching for the back door.

"Stay right there, Bowman!"

Too late, he sensed someone come up behind him. He started to swing around. Something heavy slammed into his elbow. His hand went numb. The gun fell from his fingers and he staggered forward.

"He's a cop!" Bowman yelled.

"We don't know that!" Kyra's voice came from his back as something heavy glanced off the back of his head.

Chapter Thirteen

"When I tell you to take time off, you're supposed to do it!"

Captain Walsh towered over the emergency-room cot.

"That doesn't mean interviewing victims or chasing down leads or hotdogging after suspects!"

Lucan winced. His head throbbed. His arm throbbed. In fact, he was pretty sure there wasn't a part of him that didn't hurt. He counted himself fortunate that nothing was broken. He'd even regained feeling in his hand.

"You are damn lucky not to be permanently crippled," Walsh continued, mirroring his own thoughts. "If she hadn't been injured herself, she could have done serious damage with that baseball bat. I ought to bust you back down to uniform for insubordination."

"Yes, sir. I gather they got away?"

The captain swore long and low. Behind and slightly to one side of the captain, Todd Berringer cringed.

"You are on leave. Got that? I don't want to see you for the next five days. Take him home, Berringer. And this time, O'Shay, you stay there, got it?"

The captain stalked out without waiting for his response. The nurse must have been hovering just outside because she appeared at the cubicle with his discharge papers.

"What he said," she told him acerbically. "Or I'll call your sister-in-law."

"God forbid," he muttered, signing his name. All he needed was Sally on his case. His brother Ronan's wife took no prisoners when it came to health.

Todd helped him back into his clothing, since Lucan could barely move. His head felt as if it was going to fall off if he turned it the wrong way.

"Good thing Sally is off today," Todd agreed.

"You're telling me."

"I have some good news," Todd told him as they left the hospital. "We got a lead on Bowman. A friend of his thinks he moved in with some woman he met."

"The woman have a name?"

"I'm working on it. And for the record? I never told you this. Always nice to know the captain cares, right?"

Lucan started to shake his head and thought better of the idea. "At least I didn't wreck Jessup's car."

"There is that. She said yes," he added proudly. "I'm going to take her to that new seafood place that just opened in Bethesda."

"Does she like seafood?"

His stricken expression was almost comical.

"I don't know!"

Lucan's lips twitched. "Ask Rhea Loosh. The two of them are friends."

"Oh, yeah. Right. Great! Good idea. Thanks."

"Anytime. You missed my turn."

"No, I didn't."

Lucan shifted. A jolt of pain reminded him that all movement was treacherous. "I am not going to my mother's. I want to go home."

"You sound like a little kid. I'm following the captain's orders."

"He told you to take me *home!*"

"Before we went in to see you he ordered me to take you to your mom's. I think he has a crush on her."

"Do not even go there!" The captain and his mother? It didn't bear thinking about.

"He wants to be sure you don't slip into a coma and die or something."

"I have a mild concussion and some bruises."

"I'll say. We heard the doctor tell you that you needed to be watched for the next twenty-four hours. And if you think I want a tongue-lashing like you just got, forget it, pal. The captain said take you to your mom's, and I'm taking you to your mom's."

"Did the captain forget she has three kids and Kyra staying with her? How does he think that's going to be restful? Where does he think I'm supposed to sleep?"

Todd shrugged. "I'm just the delivery man. You could always bunk down with the gorgeous Kyra." He waggled his eyebrows.

And the memory of how he had done exactly that last night snapped off anything else Lucan might have said. But he would have protested harder if he'd known his brother Ronan's car would be in his mother's driveway when they got there. Ronan's car meant Sally was probably there.

"I'll pay for your date if you'll just take me home," he pleaded with Todd.

"Sorry, pal. Besides, if your brother and his family are here, your mom probably baked something yummy. I'll help you inside."

"A year's supply of my mother's baked goods?"

"Take it like a man, Lucan."

Kyra opened the door before he could insert his key. "What happened?"

She was so beautiful. Her genuine concern settled over him like a welcome glove. "Keep your voice down," he begged, but it was too late. His nephew came charging around the corner.

"Uncle Lucan!"

"Hey, sport," he greeted.

"Wow. That's a really big bruise."

"Yeah, it is." Fortunately, the one on the back of his head wasn't visible.

"Lucan?" Kyra turned to Todd. "What happened? Where's his car?"

"The captain made Jessup reclaim it. The Lone Ranger here lost a duel with a baseball bat."

"Will you be quiet?" Lucan demanded of Todd as more of his relatives crowded into the small foyer.

"Did you say a baseball bat?" Ronan asked, coming forward.

"Too late," Todd whispered.

"Are you okay?" Ronan demanded. "You look like hell."

"Dad, you aren't supposed to say that."

"You're right. I'm sorry."

"Ronan?" Sally appeared from the kitchen, wiping her hands on a dishtowel. "Good grief, Lucan. Did you have another accident?"

Lucan closed his eyes. He was in for it now. His mother bustled over to join the others. "An' what have ye gone and done to yerself now, Lucan Alexander O'Shay?"

Lucan sighed. "Nothing."

"He was attacked with a baseball bat," Todd announced at the same time.

"When I feel better, you're a dead man," he told his friend with a pointed nod at Kip, Brian and Maggie standing behind the others.

"I'm fine," he assured his mother and everyone else. "I was checking out an empty house that turned out not to be empty."

Kyra's lips parted in distress. Of course she would figure out exactly what house he'd been checking.

"It's no big deal. I'm bruised, that's all."

Casey's three children had drawn closer together. The last thing Lucan wanted to do was upset them any further.

"Why didn't you shoot 'em, Uncle Lucan?"

"I try not to do that, Riley. There's too much paperwork involved. Does anyone mind if I sit down?"

Immediately, Sally and his mother took charge. They ordered a living room chair cleared for his use. That's when he saw the boxes of ornaments strewn about the living room. A string of lights lay glowing on the carpeting where Ronan had no doubt been checking and replacing burnt-out bulbs.

"We came to help decorate the tree," Ronan explained.

"And decorate cookies," his son put in.

"You'll be staying to dinner, Todd," his mother stated firmly.

"I don't want to put anyone out." Todd feigned reluctance.

"'Tis no bother. Sally brought a salad and I'm making spaghetti."

His eyes lit. "From scratch?"

"Well, of course. I don't hold with that processed stuff. Sure an' there's plenty to go around. You can help decorate the tree and cookies."

His mother's deepening brogue was a sure sign she was upset. Lucan tried to ease her worry. "I'd keep Todd away from the cookies if you want any left for Christmas," Lucan advised. He gave in to the chaos with as much grace as he could muster, sinking into the cleared chair gratefully.

"What happened, Lucan?" Sally persisted.

"I made a wrong assumption and got hurt. Look, Sal, it's an ongoing police investigation. I really can't talk about it."

"Let me see your discharge papers."

Sally fussed over him and went to make a phone call, probably to the nurse on duty in the ER. He watched thankfully as Ronan diverted the others with decorating preparations, but Casey's children eyed Lucan with worry.

Maggie came over clutching Bear. To his surprise, she climbed up in his lap.

"Maggie, honey—"

"It's okay, Kyra. She can sit with me." Even though it put some added strain on his sore arm, he wasn't willing to put her down when the child curled trustingly against him.

"What's this?" he asked, fingering one of the large shiny necklaces around the bear's neck.

"Aunt Kyra gave them to me."

"That's very pretty, Maggie." But he didn't miss the stricken look on Kip's face.

"She traded for that stuff we found in the closet," Brian told him.

Lucan's gaze flew to Kyra. The children had found something else in the closet?

Kyra gave a small shake of her head. Whatever was going on, she didn't want to discuss it in front of the children.

"Well, good," he told Brian and saw Kip relax a fraction.

"Because these look perfect on Bear."

Satisfied, Maggie leaned her head against his good shoulder as Ronan called Kip and Brian to come and help him. Kyra disappeared back into the kitchen and Lucan let the commotion swirl around him. Lethargy sank its talons deep. Within minutes his eyes closed and he leaned his head against the child's soft hair. He dozed lightly, listening to the familiar sounds of family chaos.

TEARS CAME TO HER eyes as Kyra studied Lucan's sleeping form. Maggie was asleep in his arms with Bear curled in hers. The scene couldn't have been more poignant.

She could love this man forever.

"Sleep. That's what he desperately needs."

Surprised, she blinked back the tears and looked at Todd. He'd taken her aside right after Lucan sat down and told her what had happened. She was still trying to get her mind around the fact that her sister had tried to kill Lucan.

"He looks good holding that little girl, doesn't he? Lucan's a family man through and through."

"Matchmaking, Todd?" She was surprised that her voice came out so evenly.

Todd's lips curved unrepentantly, but his eyes were serious. "I've known Lucan since grade school and I've seen the way he looks at you, Kyra. He's never looked at anyone else quite that way before. Not even his first wife. And if you're worried that he's pining for her, don't. That was over a long time ago with no regrets on either side."

"I know."

He blinked in surprise and then smiled. "He told you about her?"

"We had a lot of time to talk last night." Todd's stare was too perceptive. She shifted, wishing someone would call him away.

"Now why do I think there may have been more than talk involved?"

"Because you're a testosterone-driven male?" she replied mock-sweetly.

Todd laughed. "You're perfect for him."

"When you propose to your lieutenant, let's talk."

"Hey! We haven't even had a date yet."

"Precisely." And she headed back out to the kitchen. But her mind wasn't as quickly diverted. Lucan O'Shay was a cop. Her sister had just tried to kill him with a baseball bat. When they caught up with Casey and she went to jail, Kyra would be raising her three children. Talk about an auspicious start to a relationship!

Maggie and Lucan roused before dinner. She watched him covertly as he moved stiffly to wash up before joining the family at the huge dining-room table. Dinner was a noisy affair, but Lucan was quiet. He picked at his food with eyes glazed by pain. When Sally fussed over him, Lucan made more of an effort to join in the conversation, but it was obvious his heart wasn't in it. He passed on dessert, and when the women stood to clear the table, Maureen pulled her aside.

"Get him upstairs to bed, lass. He won't take it from us, but he'll listen to you."

Sally nodded. "You'll have to keep a close eye on him. It's a mild concussion, but we don't want him slipping into a coma in his sleep."

No, she definitely didn't want anything else bad to happen to Lucan O'Shay. Her guilt was already at an all-time high.

Lucan was heading for the chair again when she stopped him. "May I talk with you in private for a few minutes?"

"There's somewhere private in this madhouse?"

"My room."

"Possessive, aren't you?" but he smiled to show he was teasing. The smile didn't quite reach his pain-filled eyes.

"Sometimes."

He didn't move with his usual fluid grace, but he made it to the bedroom where he sank down on the freshly made bed.

"Ah. Alone at last. Kyra…" A different pain creased his forehead.

"I know what happened. Todd told me. Casey tried to kill you."

"No! Well, yes, but it was a misunderstanding. She didn't believe I was a cop. She thought I was one of the men who attacked her."

Her heart stuttered. "So she isn't working with Jordan?"

"I don't know. The jury is still out on that one. I was hoping she would have called you."

Stricken, Kyra ran to the dresser where she'd left her purse and fished out her cell phone. "Three missed calls! Lucan, she did try to call!"

She pressed Speaker and played the first call. "Kyra, it's Casey. Call me back, please! Something happened. I need to know where the children are. Call me!" The second message was a simple "Please call me when you get this," and the third message sounded frantic. "Kyra, where are you? Please! I need you!"

Heart pounding, she pressed her sister's cell phone number. The phone rang unanswered and transferred to voice mail.

"Casey, it's Kyra. I'm sorry. I just got your messages. I'll keep the phone with me from now on. Call me back. The kids are fine. They're safe. You'll be so proud of Kip. He's taken such good care of them. The cop you hit is going to be fine. He knows it was a misunderstanding. You aren't in trouble. Call me back, Casey. I need to see you. Your children need to see you! I'll help you, no matter what sort of trouble you're in. You're my sister. I love you." And her voice broke. Tears streamed down her cheeks. "Call me, Casey." She recited her number and hung up.

She hadn't heard Lucan come off the bed, but he drew her into his arms, holding her silently while she sobbed.

"Sorry," she muttered, striving for control as he stroked her back. "This is getting to be a bad habit."

"Me holding you?"

She gazed at him through blurry eyes. "Me crying. I like it when you hold me."

"Good. I like it too, however I really need to sit down now."

"Lucan!"

"I'm fine. Just sore."

She moved around him and pulled down the covers. "Lie down."

"I don't need to lie down."

"Do too. I'll tell your mother. And Sally."

"You'd do it, too."

She nodded, sniffing to clear her stuffy nose. "Let me get your shoes."

"Haven't we played this scene before?"

She choked on a laugh. "I forgot you have a foot fetish."

"Only where yours are concerned. You have beautiful feet."

"Feet aren't beautiful."

"Yours are."

She ignored the thrill tripping along her spine. "Get your pants off, O'Shay."

"I'm not that easy." The smile was a bit forced as he winced. "And I'm not ready for bed."

"Liar." She bent down to remove his shoes, and he nuzzled her hair. "Stop that. You're hurt."

"Not that hurt."

"I've heard that before. Besides, Sally would disagree."

"That's a low blow, Kyra."

She pulled off his last sock and stood. "We need to talk."

His demeanor changed when he recognized she was serious. Putting his gun under his pillow, Lucan loosened his belt and stood to drop his pants before sitting back down without grace.

"Kip found something."

He held her gaze. "A pendant and a ring in the closet?"

Kyra gaped. "How did you know?"

"They were taken from the murdered woman."

"Oh, my God." She was suddenly shaking. "Kip saw Jordan with them." She blurted out what her nephew had told her. "Casey doesn't know. I'm sure she doesn't know."

He nodded. "I don't think so either."

"Thank God." Relief eased some of her tension.

"We'll get the ring, Kyra. Where's the pendant?"

She pulled it from under her sweater. "I didn't want to lose it so I put it on one of my chains."

"Good grief. Gaudy-looking trinket for such a delicate chain."

"Do you know what this is worth if it's real?" she asked.

"Oh, it's real. Or at least one just like it is. The appraisal value was on the order of $700,000. I think the ring alone was $5,000. Did you tell Todd?" He started to rise and bit back a groan.

"Not yet. I didn't want to bring it up with everyone

around, but I'll find him now. Let me tell him. You really do need to take it easy."

"You may be right. Kyra, your sister is with her ex-husband."

"I know. Todd told me." She shook her head. "I can't figure that out. She was so angry with him. I'd have sworn he'd be the last person she'd turn to. He can't be involved in this, can he?"

"I don't know."

She shook her head. "It doesn't make sense. I know she loved him once, but after he started drinking he changed. That was when he became abusive. I just don't see why she'd be with him again." Her eyes narrowed. "But you can be sure I'll ask her when she calls me back."

He didn't pursue the subject. That was probably a good measure of how much pain he was in.

"Don't invite Casey here," Lucan ordered. "Try to set up a meeting someplace public. If Jordan has killed once, there's nothing to say he won't kill again and we don't want to inadvertently lead him to the kids."

"No. I understand. I'll talk to Todd and give him the pendant." She kissed him lightly and stepped away before he could take the kiss deeper. "I'll be back to check on you."

"I'm counting on that. And Kyra, I know she's your sister, but don't meet Casey alone. Promise me."

She drew in a breath and released it slowly. As much as she wanted to argue, she knew he was right. "I promise."

Everyone was still gathered around the dining-room table when she went back downstairs. But now instead of food, piles of cookies and bowls of icing with assorted containers of decorations were spread across the table. "Where's Todd?"

Ronan looked up. "He got a call and had to leave."

"He left?" She swallowed a moment of panic.

"Is something wrong?"

She fingered the pendant under her sweater. "No. No, Lucan wanted me to tell him something. Is he coming back?"

"I don't think so, but you could call him," Sally suggested before turning to her young daughter. "Honey, I think that's enough icing on that cookie. Why don't you take another one?"

"I've Todd's number," Maureen offered.

Kyra followed her into the kitchen.

"He's resting then?" Maureen asked, and Kyra knew she meant Lucan, not Todd.

"Yes, I got him to lie down."

"Good. I've a large bed. The wee one can sleep with me tonight and you can take her bed. That way if she has another bad dream I'll be there."

"Maureen, I don't know how to thank you for all you've done. For all you're doing."

"No thanks being needed." She copied a number on a slip of paper and handed it to her. "He's a good man, Kyra."

Again she had no trouble following Maureen's jump and knew she was blushing. "I know. I've told him as much."

"Your man seems nice as well."

Kyra shook her head. "He's not my man. Simon works with me. He's a friend, that's all. He caught a plane back to Boston this afternoon."

Satisfied, Maureen nodded and left Kyra staring after her. Maureen was matchmaking?

Todd didn't answer when she called his number. Kyra hesitated, but left him a quick message about the jewelry and her sister's call before she hung up. She went back upstairs to report to Lucan and found him sound asleep and looking so relaxed she envied him. Even bruised and battered, he was a good-looking man.

She left the room, closing the door softly. Until Casey or Todd called back, there was nothing more they could do.

Taking a deep breath, she rejoined the family with an outward calm she was far from feeling.

It was a relief when Ronan and Sally and their children finally left. Maggie had become tired and fretful and Maureen took her upstairs to supervise her bath, allowing Kyra to spend time with Kip and Brian.

Of the three children, Brian seemed the most resilient. He missed his mother, but he'd struck up a bond with Riley, who was close to his age, and all the commotion of the afternoon and evening had worn him out. While he took his bath she challenged Kip to a game of air hockey.

Kip worried her. He'd become silent and withdrawn. Though he played, it was obvious his heart wasn't in the game, and he headed for the bathroom as soon as his brother finished. Brian was yawning hugely and the boys went to bed without any fuss as soon as Kip finished.

Maureen was straightening the kitchen when Kyra returned downstairs. She looked so tired. Kyra felt more than a twinge of guilt.

"Maureen? I'd be happy to finish wiping the counters and cleaning the coffeepot. Why don't you go up and get some rest while you can? I'll be going upstairs shortly myself."

"That would be a blessing, lass. I confess I'm not as young as I once was. You'll check on Lucan then?"

"Before I go to bed," she promised.

Kyra took her time cleaning as the house settled and grew quiet. She loved the warmth and comfort Maureen's home projected. The lingering scents of cookies and dinner were overpowered by the fragrant scent of pine from the brightly twinkling tree when she moved into the living room. She sat on the worn couch, savoring the quiet and the blinking lights on the tree. Christmases past with her own family came to mind, and she savored the memories. Unfortunately, worry over Casey overshadowed the happier images.

She tried Casey's number again. This time she didn't leave a message when there was no answer. The feeling of peace slipped away. Lucan's warning had made her edgy. *What if* thoughts were plaguing her. If anything happened to her sister now...

Kyra refused to consider that. She rose and unplugged the tree, turning off the inside and outside lights and pausing to stare out at the street. Light snow was falling again. Nothing else moved save the twinkling white Christmas lights across the street.

Her mind flitted from one thought to another. She needed to go shopping. Whatever else happened, she wanted to give Maureen something special for Christmas.

And Lucan? That gift would be trickier. She needed something personal without being *too* personal. She'd have to walk a fine line with his selection. Sighing, she turned and headed for the stairs.

A noise in the kitchen stopped her with one foot on the bottom step. Had she forgotten to turn something off?

She started to reverse direction when an icy breeze swept down the hall. Her lips parted. Belatedly, she realized what the sound had been. Someone had just opened the kitchen door.

Chapter Fourteen

Instinct sent her flying up the steps. It could be one of Lucan's brothers, but everyone seemed to use the front door. And they wouldn't have been so furtive. Rushing into the bedroom, she nearly fell over Kip in the dark.

Lucan was already on his feet, yanking up his pants and reaching for his gun.

"Someone's out there!" the boy whispered shrilly.

"They're in the house," she corrected.

"Where?" Lucan demanded.

"Kitchen."

"Stay here. Both of you."

He left the room on that command, silent as a breeze. Kyra turned to the dresser, fumbling in the dark for her purse.

"What are you doing?" Kip asked.

"Getting my... Here it is." She felt the shape with her fingers.

"What's that?"

"Pepper spray. How did you know someone was out there, Kip?"

"I was looking out the window. I saw someone creeping around the yard so I came to tell Lucan."

Kip's bedroom faced the back of the house.

"Good work." She felt for the telephone on the small

desk, picked it up and dialed 911. She had time to tell the dispatcher they had an intruder before a shot shattered the quiet.

"Shots fired," she reported, no longer trying to be quiet. "A police officer needs help." More shots followed in close succession.

"Lucan!" Kip shouted.

Kyra dropped the phone and tried to grab for the boy as he ran into the hall. She stopped him when he would have started down the stairs. Brian's door opened across from them.

"Brian!" she called, holding Kip as Maureen's door opened at the far end of the hall.

The older woman stood silhouetted in a nightgown, holding a huge revolver. "To me, lass," she ordered.

Kyra herded the boys in her direction. "There's someone in the house. Lucan went down to confront him."

"In with you. Lucan will handle him. Go stand in the closet with your sister," she ordered the boys.

"Again?" Brian complained as Maureen closed the bedroom door.

"Is that loaded?" Kyra whispered.

"Wouldn't be worth a lick of salt if it wasn't, now would it, lass? My Mitchell, God rest his soul, believed in being prepared. I'm accounted a fair shot. Now you littles get in there an' keep down."

"Lucan might be hurt!" Kip protested.

"Don't ye be frettin' over my Lucan. 'Tis the intruder should be doin' the worryin'. This one picked the wrong house and no mistake." She glanced at Kyra. "Pepper spray, is it? A gun would be better."

"I have one, but Lucan took my bullets."

She tsked. "An' I hope he won't be regrettin' that decision."

Maureen's bedroom faced the front of the house, so the boys raced to the windows as sirens screamed down the street. Neither Kyra nor Maureen bothered to corral them.

The cruisers' flashing lights overshadowed the Christmas lights across the street as uniformed officers converged on the house.

Maureen crossed to her closet and replaced her gun in a cabinet, locking it. "No sense addin' to the confusion," she explained. "The police can handle it from here. I'd be putting that out of sight as well."

Kyra shoved the pepper spray in a pocket.

"Where's Lucan?" Kip demanded of the first officer to arrive.

"Who?" The officer looked to Kyra.

"Detective Lucan O'Shay. This is his mother and this is her house. Lucan went downstairs to confront the intruder and someone started shooting."

"We swept the downstairs, ma'am. There isn't anyone there. But the kitchen door is wide open."

"The idiot! He's hurt and he doesn't even have shoes on! He'll have pneumonia." Kyra flew down the stairs. Lucan wouldn't have gone far in bare feet. But if the police hadn't seen him… Fear for him filled her as she hit the end of the stairs where she paused when she heard the deep rumble of his voice coming from the kitchen.

"If I'd had shoes on, he wouldn't have gotten away."

She scooted past another officer to where he stood. His face and hands were red from the cold and he was shivering hard.

"Idiot! Captain Walsh told you to rest. Why did you chase him?"

He turned. Somehow she was in his arms. He pulled her tight against his cold body, returning her fierce hug. "Everyone's okay?"

"Of course. *We* didn't go outside barefoot in the cold chasing after a man with a gun. Lucan, how did he find us here?"

Lucan scowled. "He must have been watching your

sister's place. He probably followed Todd and me here after the attack."

"Did you wound him at least?"

His lips curved. "You never fail to surprise me."

She drew back far enough to glare at him. "I protect what's mine, O'Shay, and you should be sitting down."

The children and his mother crowded into the kitchen with them. "Brian, would you be after fetchin' his socks and shoes for me? There's a good lad."

"Just the socks, Brian," he corrected his mother.

"We heard you shoot at him. Did you get him?" Kip asked.

"No. But about that." He turned to his mother. "We're going to have to do some replastering, I'm afraid. And I hope you weren't overly fond of that red cookie jar."

THE MORNING BROUGHT OVERCAST skies once more. It also brought colder temperatures and Todd Berringer. There was an aura of excitement about him as he relayed the captain's request for Lucan and Kyra to come to the station. Todd even turned down a homemade sticky bun.

"What's going on?" Lucan asked.

Todd glanced at the children who'd gathered around. "The captain needs to see you both right away."

Kyra didn't hesitate. "I'll get my purse and coat."

Lucan followed her example, glad he had arranged for Ronan and Neil to take the kids to a movie and back to Neil and Phyllis's house afterwards. Flynn had planned to take his mother and Whitney Christmas shopping. Lucan wanted to keep everyone away from the house until this situation was resolved. Phyllis bravely offered to fix dinner for the entire family.

"I'll not be chased out of my home by a bully with a gun," his mother had asserted when Lucan suggested she go and stay with one of his brothers. "If that idiot is daft enough to return, we'll show him the error of his ways."

Budging a mountain was easier than moving his mother once she set her mind to something.

Kyra had been fretting over the fact that her sister still hadn't called. Lucan tried not to let her see how worried he was as well.

As they left the house, Todd's first words changed everything. "We have Casey and Milt Bowman."

"What?"

"Why didn't you tell me?" Kyra asked at the same time. "Is my sister all right?"

"When did you pick them up?"

Todd held up a hand. "Hey, one at a time. I got a call last night at your house. Someone spotted Bowman's car on a street in Adams Morgan. Turns out he's staying with a girlfriend who has a place there. Your sister was staying with them."

Kyra and Lucan exchanged a startled glance.

"We picked them up this morning when they headed out for breakfast. Casey's asking for Kyra and her children."

"She's okay?"

"A little the worse for wear, but she'll be fine and she has quite a story to tell. Seems Fillmont did call her from the golf course on Sunday and told her someone was trying to kill him. He warned her they might come to the house looking for him, but she didn't have time to get the kids away before the power went out. So she put the kids in the safe room Fillmont had installed, thinking they wouldn't hurt her. And other than a few slaps, they didn't. But they ransacked the place looking for money they said Fillmont owed them."

Lucan nodded. "They were looking for the ring and pendant."

"I think so, too. They spent a lot of time pawing through her jewelry. When they couldn't find anything, they forced Casey at gunpoint to go with them."

Kyra sent Lucan another quick look.

"They tied her up and locked her in the basement of a house in D.C.," Todd continued. "But your sister's pretty resourceful. She eventually worked her way loose, got out of the basement and snuck out the back door. One of the cars in the driveway was unlocked with the ignition wires dangling. She managed to get it started. Unfortunately, the men heard her and came after her."

"How would Casey know how to do that?" Kyra asked.

Todd grinned. "She said she saw it done in a movie once." He pulled into the lot at the precinct house.

"She lost the men on the Beltway and headed for home but took an off ramp too fast and lost control of the car. When she came to, she was trapped. She says she doesn't remember much about the accident or getting free or climbing back up the embankment and the next thing she knew, she was in the hospital."

"Where your officers bullied her," Kyra accused.

"Manacuzzi was pretty rough on her," Todd agreed. "And she was afraid they were going to arrest her for stealing the car. When he started in about the money we found in the house, she panicked."

"She just wanted to get to her kids," Kyra protested.

"I know. As soon as she could, she called Bowman's cell phone and asked him to come get her. Unfortunately, the ice storm started. He was going to drive her home but the roads were too bad so he took her to his place instead."

"Bet his new girlfriend wasn't happy about that."

Kyra glared at Lucan for his comment.

"Actually," Todd told them, "according to your sister, the three of them have become pretty friendly. She says the girlfriend got Bowman into treatment for his alcohol addiction and helped him find a new job. She even pushed Bowman to get back in touch with Casey and start paying child support. In return, he wants visitation rights."

"Then why did he try to run when Lucan found him at the house?" Kyra demanded.

"Casey's the one who hit me," Lucan reminded her.

Todd nodded. "Bowman was horrified when she clunked you one. Casey swears she didn't believe you were really a cop. She thought you were with the men who kidnapped her."

Kyra's expression hardened. "Is she under arrest? Does she have a lawyer?"

"She waived her right to a lawyer. She's been cooperating with us."

"She knows better than that! As of now I'm representing her. And as her counsel, I don't want her saying another word until I talk to her."

"Kyra," Lucan began.

"I mean it, Lucan. Not another word. I want to see her."

"That's why you're here," Todd agreed.

CASEY FILLMONT WAS SITTING in a holding cell drinking coffee when they walked in after speaking with Captain Walsh. Casey nearly overturned her chair in her rush to greet her sister. Despite her badly bruised face and one arm in a sling, the two women still looked remarkably alike. Even their hairstyles were similar. Lucan could easily understand how Kyra had been mistaken for Casey.

But once the emotion of the first few minutes had calmed down, it was Kyra who took charge as if she were the older sister. "Don't say another word about what happened," she cautioned Casey. "Not a syllable until after you've spoken with me privately. I'm going on record as your lawyer."

"Can you do that?"

"Yes."

"But I hit a cop!"

"Quiet! Not another word."

Casey looked past her to Lucan. "Ohmigod, he's the one I—"

"Quiet, Casey! This is Detective Lucan O'Shay. He's been helping me try to find you."

"I'm so sorry. Really. I thought—"

"Casey!" Kyra admonished.

Lucan nearly smiled. "It's all right, counselor. I'm fine, Mrs. Fillmont."

"You can't be. You look worse than I do," she argued. "Did I do that to your face?"

Kyra rolled her eyes. Lucan did smile then. Casey's concern was genuine.

"No, ma'am. I was in a car wreck before you hit me."

"Ohmigod. That makes it worse! I'm so sorry! It was an accident!"

"I understand." And he did. Just watching her reaction to her sister had been enough to convince Lucan that Casey wasn't involved in the robberies let alone murder. Only, he was a cop, and as a cop he had to deal with evidence. He was thankful that the captain and the D.A. agreed that they didn't have anything to tie her directly to the crime. Still, Lucan was going to have to find the person who was guilty and prove it.

"Lucan, I'm formally requesting some private time with my client," Kyra announced.

"Sounds good. Why don't we take her over to Neil's place. You two can talk after dinner. I imagine Casey would like to see her children."

"Yes, please!" Casey's eyes welled with tears.

Kyra appeared stunned. "You aren't going to hold her?"

"We aren't charging her with anything right now, no. In fact, Captain Walsh is releasing a car for me to use, so if you're ready to go, we can leave."

Casey hesitated. "What about Milt? He didn't do anything wrong, and they arrested him and his girlfriend."

"There are no charges pending against Mr. Bowman and Ms. Pretermyer. They've already been released."

Casey limped over and threw her good arm around Lucan, hugging him tight. Manfully, he tried not to groan as muscles protested where her cast dug into him.

"Thank you so much, Detective. I really am sorry I hit you."

Kyra sighed audibly. Her sister stepped back allowing him to breathe again. "I believe you," he told her. "Ready to go?"

Kyra followed him to the door as Casey began pumping her for information on the children. She swung between tears and laughter while Kyra related their adventures.

Neil's house was quiet when they arrived. The children were still at the movies, but Phyllis was there with the baby. She welcomed them like old friends and after a few minutes, Lucan stepped outside to call Todd. He was still standing out front when his brother's car pulled up with Ronan and all the kids.

"What are you doing here?" Ronan asked.

Lucan smiled broadly. "I have a surprise for Kip, Brian and Maggie."

The three came to attention.

Brian looked up eagerly. "What?"

"It's inside."

Kip got out of the car and hesitated.

"Your Aunt Kyra is inside, too, Kip," he added.

The boy searched Lucan's face and nodded acceptance. Before they got halfway to the front door it opened. Casey stepped outside.

Kip stopped dead. "Mom? Mommy?"

The three children pelted across the grass. Casey held out her good arm to welcome them.

"Nice work, big brother," Ronan said softly as the rest of the kids exited the car.

Casey was laughing and crying and all four were trying to talk at once. Lucan's gaze went to Kyra. She stood inside the door wiping at the tears running down her cheeks.

"Sometimes, it's good to be a cop," he told his brothers.

Neil clapped him on the shoulder. "Let's get everyone inside before they freeze."

It was much later when Kyra drew Lucan into an unoccupied room and threw her arms around his neck. She kissed him exuberantly. "Thank you."

He continued to hold her when she would have stepped back.

"Someone might come in," she whispered.

"Let them." They were both breathing hard when he finally let her go. "You're welcome," he added with a smile. "But I don't deserve any credit. Todd found her."

Flustered, Kyra stepped away from him. "I'll kiss him later."

"You do and I'll have to punch his lights out."

Her startled expression exactly matched his own surprise at the words that had fallen from his lips.

"Tell me you didn't just say that."

Ruefully, he shrugged. "I'm having a bit of trouble believing it myself."

Kyra eyed him sternly. "You aren't going to go all neanderthal on me, are you?"

"Wasn't planning on it. On the other hand, I protect what's mine as well."

Her eyes widened. Mixed emotions crossed her face. She settled on stern.

"That sounds a tad possessive, O'Shay."

"Feels that way, too," he agreed. "Hey," he held up his palms, "it's scaring me as much as it is you. I don't do possessive."

"Ha!" she scoffed. "You're an alpha male and a cop. Of course you do possessive."

He shook his head. "I never have before." That seemed to rattle her.

"Then I suggest you don't start with me." She crossed

her arms over her chest. "I dragged you in here for a reason, O'Shay."

"Sadly, I think there's too much family around for that."

She gave him a forbidding look. "I'm serious, Lucan."

"So am I." His lips curved ruefully. "But go ahead, I'm listening."

"I want to act as a decoy to lure the killers in."

His smile vanished. "No."

"You haven't even heard me out."

"The answer's no. These guys aren't playing around, Kyra. They've already killed once and they want your sister dead."

"Exactly. You can't protect her forever, nor can she and the kids run and hide forever."

"You are *not* playing decoy."

Angrily, she faced him, hands fisted on her slim hips. "One night in my bed doesn't give you any rights, Detective."

"We didn't make it as far as a bed as I recall, and this isn't a matter of rights, it's common sense!"

"We'll see what Captain Walsh has to say!"

"Kyra…Oh!" Casey came to a halt in the doorway. "Am I interrupting something?"

"No. I was just leaving," Kyra told her sister without taking her gaze from Lucan's.

Lucan sensed excitement in her sister's banked expression.

"What's wrong, Casey?"

Casey looked from one to the other and settled on Lucan. "Jordan just tried to call me." She held out her cell phone.

Lucan took it, noting the number.

"That's his cell phone number," Casey explained. "There were half a dozen calls from him. This time he left a message. He wants me to call him back. What should I do?"

Lucan thought fast. "Set up a meeting with him."

"Absolutely not!" Kyra interrupted. "The man is a killer! You are not putting my sister at risk!"

Casey had blanched. Lucan could see she was frightened at the very idea. "I don't want you to actually meet him. I want you to call him back and arrange to meet him."

"Maybe he doesn't want to meet me," Casey protested weakly.

"He probably doesn't."

"He wants the money that was in the house and the jewelry that can tie him to the murder," Kyra interjected.

"Jewelry?" Casey asked weakly.

Lucan nodded agreement. "I've already turned it in, but he doesn't know that. All he knows is that if he goes down for this, he'll never get out of prison again."

"He's probably only still hanging around because he's broke," Kyra offered. "Call him back."

Casey blanched. "But I wouldn't know what to say!"

"Tell him you're staying with friends and you want a divorce," Lucan suggested.

"He won't care about that," Kyra protested.

"No, he won't," Lucan agreed. "But the point is, if she can act like he doesn't matter at all and implies she's going out of the country, he'll think *she* found the money."

Kyra's eyes widened. "But then he'll come after her!"

"He'll agree to meet her," Lucan corrected. "And we'll be waiting. You can do this, Casey."

The woman surprised him by nodding. "If it means getting that bastard out of my life for good, I'll do whatever I can to help you."

"Casey! No! You have the kids to think about!"

"That's exactly what I am thinking about. I have to get my children out of this situation."

"Then let me take your place," Kyra offered.

"He'll know you aren't me," Casey protested.

Kyra shook her head. "Not from a distance, he won't. He doesn't know you were injured. No one does."

As much as it went against his every instinct, Lucan

knew Kyra was right. If Casey set Jordan up, Kyra could lure him in. But it was dangerous.

He held her gaze for a long second. "You aren't going to take any unnecessary risks," Lucan insisted.

She nodded quickly, seeing his capitulation. "Call your captain. Let's set this up."

CASEY CALLED JORDAN BACK from the captain's office the first thing Monday morning. Kyra was impressed by her sister's acting ability. She'd been coached carefully, of course, but Casey had the smug tone of voice down just right. Even Kyra could believe Casey had found the money and was planning to keep it for herself.

Casey explained that she'd taken the children and left after Jordan had called to warn her. When she returned home she found the house trashed. She decided to quit her job and take the kids somewhere warm for Christmas. And by the way, she wanted a divorce. She intended to make some sweeping changes in her life. Whatever Jordan was involved in, she wanted no part of him or the police. Jordan could have everything in the house except the passports. She was going back to pick them up in a little while. He begged her to meet him and she refused, cutting him off and telling him goodbye.

Walsh congratulated her. "Nicely done, Mrs. Fillmont."

Flushed, Casey nodded before turning to her sister. "Are you sure you want to do this? Maybe I could—"

"Not a chance," Kyra interrupted. "You need to get back to the kids. They're going to be anxious every time you leave them for some time to come."

"They'll have to get over it. Assuming I still have a job after this, I have to work."

"There's a ten-thousand dollar reward for the person who helps us find those responsible for the murder of Shereen Nestler," the captain interjected. "Her husband put up the money, and I think you'll qualify."

"Oh!" Casey's expression brightened. "I could take the holidays off then."

"You can anyhow," Kyra assured her. "I'll help with any bills."

"I can't ask you—"

"You aren't asking. I'm offering."

"I believe the insurance company is also offering a reward for the necklace and ring you turned in," Captain Walsh added.

Kyra grinned. "There. See? We'll be fine. How soon before you want me to go over to the house?" She carefully did not look at Lucan. She knew he still didn't like the idea, but he'd helped set up the plan despite his concern for her safety.

Kyra loved that he cared. She was glad to see that while he wanted to protect her, he was still willing to let her take risks. Loving him was easy. She was starting to believe he felt the same way. But she wouldn't put up with someone trying to run her life. Simon had already tried that.

"I'm going over with the team now," Lucan told her. "Give us thirty minutes, then you go in. The plan is to nab him outside before he ever reaches the front door. However, the best-laid plans can go wrong for reasons no one foresees. Keep your pepper spray where you can grab it just in case. If he gets close enough to see you, he's going to realize you aren't Casey."

"So what? Even if he does, he's going to want to talk to me to find out where she is."

Lucan nodded, holding her gaze. "That's why you're going to wear a wire as well. We're covering all contingencies. But I still want you to be careful."

He gazed at her steadily. Her heart turned over. Then he turned and walked out the door. Kyra stared after him.

"He isn't going with you?" Casey asked anxiously.

"No. Lucan's going to sit in the command unit with the lieutenant in charge," Todd replied. "He'll be able to hear anything she says, but she won't be able to hear him. You okay with this, Kyra?"

"Fine. I'm fine." Lucan wasn't leaving her. He'd be there, a shout away. She tossed back her head. "Let's get the wire on."

Thirty minutes later her nerves were jumping as she pulled into her sister's driveway and got out of her sister's car. If Jordan had arrived ahead of her, they would have taken him down and called it off.

Without looking around to try and spot the hovering officers, Kyra headed straight for the front door. Her heart beat a rapid tattoo as she stepped inside.

Even knowing there were officers all around out of sight, there was a sick feeling in the pit of her stomach. The house was so silent, so dark and gloomy. Evidence of the earlier destruction was still everywhere.

Kyra wandered aimlessly about the rooms downstairs, silently urging Jordan to hurry and get this over with. She couldn't think of him as Ronnie White. And his name didn't matter. If only he'd hurry and take the bait, Casey and the kids could not live in fear for the rest of their lives.

Kyra decided she should probably make a pretext of gathering up items her sister might want, but her concentration was shot. She wandered into the kitchen. The high heels on her boots clicked loudly in the silence. She opened cupboards aimlessly, staring at the meager contents they had salvaged. She doubted there was anything in here her sister would truly want.

Opening the refrigerator without thought, she stilled. It should have been empty. Instead, an open six pack of beer, cold cuts, cheese, bread, lettuce, tomatoes, onions...

Fear twisted her insides. "Uh, Lucan, there's food in the refrigerator." The police wouldn't have put this here. "I think someone has been living in the house."

She shut the door and turned. A man with a gun stood in

the open basement doorway. He shushed her with a shake of his head and a finger to his lips.

Kyra had barely glimpsed him at the mall that day, but when he crossed to her side, she knew this was the same man who had chased after her and Kip. His eyes were deadly cold hard slits. There wasn't a doubt in her mind that he would pull the trigger before she could draw her next breath.

"Good," he whispered. "Don't make another sound."

She could smell the onion and beer on his breath.

"You're going to get me out of here and take me to your husband."

He thought she was Casey! She prayed Lucan was hearing this. Dare she tell them he had the gun aimed at her head? The bulletproof vest under her clothes wasn't going to do a thing to save her if he fired now, and her pepper spray might just as well be out in the car.

"Jordan's coming here," she told him, following his example and whispering. Her voice didn't break although she was visibly shaking.

"You're wearing a wire, right?"

Kyra didn't hesitate. "Yes." Lying to this man would definitely get her killed and no doubt he heard her talking to Lucan.

He raised his voice. "The first gun I see, we're both going to die."

She stiffened. An officer in full gear had appeared in the doorway to the dining room. "Don't do anything! Do what he says," she ordered, amazed at how calm she sounded.

The man holding the gun to her head regarded the officer. "You heard the lady. Drop your gun."

There was a split second's hesitation before the officer dropped his weapon.

"Kick it toward the table and back away. I only want White."

"You can have him," she vowed.

He snorted a surprised laugh, but his eyes remained colder than the Antarctic. "You've got guts, lady, I'll give you that. She's my ticket out of here," he said loudly, probably for the people listening to her wire. "Now, back into the living room," he told the cop. "Move!"

The man moved out of sight.

"Okay, Mrs. Fillmont. We're going to walk out of here. The next gun I see pointed my way is going to mean your death. This trigger has a very light pull. If they shoot me, they kill you as well."

"I believe you." And she did. "Lucan, you heard him? No guns. We're walking out."

A smile flitted past his lips. "You know, I'd really hate to have to kill you. Let's hope no one is feeling stupidly heroic."

She started to take a step and heard the front door open. He pulled her tight to his chest. "Sorry, sweetheart."

There were several moves she could probably make to counter this hold, but she fully believed he'd shoot her before she could get away. Kyra froze.

"Casey?"

Jordan's voice caused the man's grip to tighten even further. How had the cops let Jordan get inside?

"Answer him," the man prodded. And why hadn't they searched the house before setting up and trapping this man inside with her?

"In the kitchen, Jordan." She used the distraction to slide her hand into her pocket and grip the pepper spray. If she was incredibly lucky, she might get one chance at this.

LUCAN THOUGHT HIS HEART would stop when he heard a masculine whisper and Kyra's reply. The car at the corner reported a man matching Fillmont's description approaching on foot from the side street.

Lucan left the van, breaking cover to run through the neighbor's backyard toward the back door. Kyra would be killed along with Jordan the moment the man inside thought he could get away clean. As he ran, Lucan prayed as he never had before. If Kyra was killed he wasn't sure he could survive. He loved the stubborn, reckless woman. He wanted a chance to tell her so.

He waved back the officers in full gear who started toward him. He made his way silently onto the porch. They had left the back door unlocked so officers could move in when told to do so. He eased it open.

"Answer him," the man's voice demanded from inside.

"In the kitchen, Jordan," Kyra replied.

With no warning there was a *pfft* of sound as a silencer spoke.

Lucan had time to see Jordan falling. To bring his own weapon up even as Kyra brought her hand from her pocket and the man started turning his gun back toward her. She fired point blank in his face. He jerked his head back with a startled yell.

Lucan fired. So did a uniformed officer now standing in the dining-room doorway to the side of him.

And so did the man with the gun.

Kyra dropped to her knees on the floor.

Chapter Fifteen

Lucan rushed to Kyra, coughing and choking at the potent fumes from the pepper spray filling the room. Tears streamed from her tightly closed eyes. She was alive!

His own eyes began to burn as Lucan pulled her into his arms, barely noticing the officers in full gear rushing into the room. He carried Kyra to the back porch away from the potent fumes.

"Where are you hit?" he demanded.

"I'm not."

He offered up a quick thankful prayer. "Blink as much as you can. You need tears to wash out the chemical." He followed his own advice.

An officer appeared with water and a wet dishrag. "Wash your skin off wherever the spray touched and don't rub it," he advised. "Reggie," he called to someone inside, "Get me some ice. The ice will give you a little relief until the effects dissipate. Looks like it got you, too, Detective. You should have had full gear on."

"She didn't."

His eyes burned like fury, but Lucan squinted through his tears and tended to Kyra.

"I can't see!"

"It's okay. The capillaries in your eyes are dilated. Keep blinking! The effects dissipate after about forty-five min-

utes. Hold still while I pour this water in your eyes. We want
to flush them out."

"Did they get him?" she gasped. "Jordan. Did they get
him?"

"I've no idea. Try to relax."

"I'm trying! God, that burns."

"Tell me about it. I told you this was a bad plan."

She took a half-hearted swipe in his direction.

Todd showed up to inform him that both men inside
were dead. Lucan felt no remorse as he and the other officer
who'd fired surrendered their weapons for ballistics testing.
Paramedics arrived to treat them, but both he and Kyra
refused a ride to the hospital.

Her face was red and puffy, and her eyes, when she could
finally open them, were swollen a fiery red that was painful
to look at. Still, Lucan counted them both extremely lucky.
His hand seldom lost contact with her to reassure himself
she was alive and basically unharmed.

Eventually, Todd volunteered to run them home.

"My house," Lucan commanded. "Not my mother's."
He thought Kyra might argue, but she didn't say a word.

"No problem. The captain didn't say anything except that
I should give you a lift home. But you might want to let your
mom know you're both okay. I'm sure Flynn heard the am-
bulance call."

"I'll call her."

Kyra was unnaturally silent. Lucan hoped it was because
her eyes still smarted, but he didn't think so. Was she upset
with him? There was a good chance it was his shot that had
killed a man today. He regretted the necessity, but there had
been no other choice. She had to know that.

Then again, she was probably upset because it had been
her idea to lure her brother-in-law into the trap that had
resulted in his death. Kyra was a sensitive woman for such
a strong person. Was she regretting her choice?

"You should take a shower," he told her once they were inside his house. "Wash your hair to make sure you get all the pepper spray cleaned off. I'll wipe your coat down for you."

"Thanks." She handed him her coat and headed for the stairs. "I need to call my sister."

"Captain Walsh will tell her what happened."

"She should hear it from me first."

"Kyra? Are you all right?"

She turned with a troubled expression. "It isn't over."

"What do you mean?"

"Two men shot at me the other night. That means there's another one still out there, and now we can't ask Jordan who he is."

KYRA'S THOUGHTS CONTINUED to spin as she toweled her hair dry and put her clothes back on. Casey had sounded relieved when they'd spoken, but Kyra knew the grief and anger would come once her sister had time to think about everything.

While she had Casey on the phone, Kyra had pumped her for information about Jordan's friends.

"I only met a couple of the people he worked with. I know he hung out with Robby Krinegolt a lot. He runs errands and stuff at the country club. He's called the house a few times, but I don't really know who else."

Kyra studied her reflection in the mirror. Her eyes still looked irritated, but there was nothing she could do about that. She headed downstairs to talk to Lucan.

He'd cleaned out the fireplace and was setting logs on the grate to light a fire. She watched the play of muscles beneath his shirt as he worked. For a lean man, he was surprisingly strong. He'd lifted her back at her sister's house as if she'd weighed nothing at all. And that had to have cost him. He was hurt, after all. But there was strength in his character as well as his body.

Lucan could be bossy and arrogant in his cop mode, but tender and loving otherwise. She'd watched him interact with her niece and her nephews as well as his own family. All the children adored him.

She adored him.

He'd been divorced for years now. Was he willing to try again?

Was she actually thinking in terms of marriage and forever? With Lucan?

He turned and saw her. "Hey."

There was welcome and tenderness in the look he gave her.

"Hey yourself. Planning to light that?"

"That depends." He watched her closely. "You planning to stay?"

He wasn't only asking about her immediate intentions and she knew it. Kyra drew in a breath. She held his gaze and nodded. "I'm planning to stay."

"C'mere."

She smiled. "How about I meet you halfway?"

Laugh lines appeared in the corners of his eyes. He dusted off his hands. "Sounds perfect."

"You know, one of these times we'll have to try this in a bed," Lucan grumbled, reaching for his pants.

"Just for the sheer novelty?"

"Precisely."

He watched her step into her panties and felt a shaft of renewed desire.

"Get that look out of your eyes," she warned.

"What look?"

She glanced down at his pants. "*That* look. We have a few other things to take care of first."

Tilting his head in question at the serious expression on her face, he waited. "Like what?"

"We need to find out who Robby Krinegolt is."

The name was familiar but he couldn't immediately place it. "Who?"

"Someone who works at the country club. Casey told me Jordan hung out with him."

That brought him to his feet. "Why didn't you mention this before?"

"I intended to, but you sidetracked me, if you'll recall. Do you know who he is?"

Lucan nodded. "Yeah, I met him. Mid twenties, five-eleven, brown hair, small scar on his left cheek. He's a bartender, waiter, errand boy."

"Casey said Jordan hung out with him. He even called the house a few times. Do you think he could have been working with Jordan?" She pulled on her sweater.

"It's worth checking him out." Lucan was already reaching for his cell phone.

"This better be a friendly call," Todd warned as he answered. "I'm off duty."

"Put in for overtime. White was friends with Robby Krinegolt at the country club. I think he may be the second man who shot at Kyra."

"What?"

"Pick me up. I'll explain on the way. I need to call and get an address on him." He disconnected and called the Oak Forest Country Club. The woman who answered told him they were closed for the day and Mr. Ventner wasn't there. When Lucan persisted, his assistant, Ralph Montgomery, agreed to take the call.

Lucan identified himself and explained what he wanted.

"Is there a problem, Detective? Robby's an excellent employee."

"No. Just routine. I need to ask him a few questions."

Montgomery sounded concerned, but he gave Lucan an address in Olney. By the time Lucan finished, Kyra was nowhere in sight. He found her completely dressed and puttering around in the kitchen making coffee.

Lucan walked up behind her and slid his arms around her waist. Pulling her against him, he kissed the top of her head.

"You should probably eat something before you leave," she told him, snuggling into the embrace.

Holding her felt so right Lucan hated to release her. She turned to face him. "There's no time," he told her. "Todd will be here shortly." He tensed, watching her face closely. "Will you be here when I get back?"

"Oh, I expect so. I called Casey. Your mother is certain you're going to starve to death if she doesn't feed you so she's coming by with a meal." There was a twinkle in her eye as she added, "She offered to bring my nightgown and a change of clothing. I think my sister was scandalized."

Relief flooded him. Kyra wasn't upset that he was leaving. "Are you scandalized as well?"

"Not really. Maybe a little surprised, but Maureen's house is getting a bit crowded. I don't think she realized what she was taking on when she invited the Wolfstead clan to move in with her."

"I wouldn't be so sure of that. I think she's matchmaking. My mother likes you."

"Your mother would probably like anyone willing to take on the care and feeding of her last unmarried son. She's probably tired of sending you care packages all the time."

He grinned back at her. "There is that." He sobered. "I don't know how soon I'll be back."

Her hand caressed his cheek. "I'm not going anywhere. If I fall asleep you can wake me. Maybe we'll even give your bed a try."

Relief swept him. She wasn't angry. She understood. Or was it because she had a personal stake in this case?

She kissed him lightly. "Go get your man, Detective."

He stood very still. Searching her expression, he saw

only love there. He remembered the last time a woman had looked at him like that, but Kyra wasn't Bess. A car horn honked out front.

"I believe that's your ride, Detective." She brushed his mouth with her lips. "You'd better go."

"Yes." He needed to go.

THE ADDRESS IN OLNEY was a house that belonged to Robby's mother. A heavy-set woman with a perpetual scowl answered the door.

"Good afternoon, ma'am." Lucan flipped open his badge. "I'm Detective—"

She didn't even glance at it. "If you're looking for Robby go around to the back. He lives in the basement and he has his own door so his friends don't bother me." She glared at the two of them.

"Yes, ma'am, we—"

"I don't go down there," she interrupted.

"We just—"

She went on as if he hadn't tried to speak. "But he isn't home. You can see his van's gone." She nodded toward the rutted driveway. "I heard his phone ring a while ago."

"Do you know—"

"You can go and wait if you want."

"Uh, we were hoping—"

"My show's coming on. I have to go."

Lucan and Todd exchanged looks as she shut the door in their faces. "Thank you, ma'am," he told the door.

"Pleasant sort," Todd commented. "Think that last comment was an invitation for us to go in and have a look around?"

"I think it could be loosely interpreted that way."

Sliding-glass doors had been replaced with a traditional door. The deadbolt hadn't been set so it was easy to pop it open. The basement was a mess. It was quite obvious from the takeout-food wrappers, cans of soda and beer scattered around that Mrs. Krinegolt really meant it when she said she never came down here. In one corner was a stack of items Lucan was pretty sure would match the things stolen in the last two robberies. Among them was a monogrammed set of golf clubs.

"The initials match the Fisk job," Todd told him as he strolled among the debris looking for whatever he could find. "I think we hit pay dirt."

"In more ways than one," Lucan confirmed. "Never underestimate the stupidity of a criminal." He held up a pad of paper sitting beside the telephone. While he didn't recognize the number, he recognized the name written beneath it. Paul Atteril was a known fence.

Todd shook his head. "This is too easy. We need to get out and call it in."

Lucan nodded absently. There was a scribbled notation beneath Paul's name. Apprehension chased down his spine at the words.

Jordan caught? Find the woman!

"What's wrong, Lucan?"

Lucan grabbed the phone. He scrolled through the caller ID to see who the last caller had been. His heart sank, unsurprised to see Oak Forest come up.

"There may be another player." Lucan handed him the pad of paper. "Montgomery called and warned him."

"Ventner's assistant?"

"Yeah. He reluctantly gave me the address when I told him I was looking for Robby. We need to get someone to my mother's place right now!"

FULL DARK HAD SETTLED over the street before Casey and Maureen arrived bearing leftovers. Technically, Maureen arrived at Lucan's house with the food since Casey only had the one arm and was still limping painfully thanks to her bad knee. As Kyra helped them carry the food inside, they explained they'd left the children playing board games with Lucan's brother and sister-in-law.

"Who are we feeding here? An army?"

"Have ye not seen my lads tuck into a meal?" Maureen asked.

"Point taken. I don't know what's in this casserole, but it smells great. Lucan had to go out for a bit, but he should be back shortly."

Maureen's forehead pleated. "Does the man never stop? He's supposed to be resting."

Kyra smiled and shrugged. "He's a cop."

"An' that doesn't bother you?"

"Being in a somewhat related line of work myself, I understand. Cops can't punch a clock like some people."

"Bess didn't like it."

Kyra remembered that was the name of Lucan's first wife. "People need different things in their lives, Maureen. Being a cop is what Lucan loves. I'm fine with that."

Maureen's smile took years off her face. "I've waited a long time for him to find someone like you, lass."

Kyra felt a blush staining her cheeks. She wasn't sure exactly how to respond so she settled for a simple, "Thank you."

"You aren't serious about Lucan?" Casey protested. "I mean, he's a great guy and everything, but I nearly killed him with Kip's baseball bat!"

"The stuff family legends are made of," Maureen told her cheerfully.

Kyra smiled. "I love him."

Her sister gaped. "You just met him. And you hate arrogant, bossy men! He's a cop! Those traits come with the badge."

"And can be put aside when the badge comes off."

"And I'm thinkin' my Lucan has met his match with your sister," Maureen stated.

"But she's only known him a few days!"

"True," Kyra agreed.

"I knew the moment I clamped eyes on my Mitchell that I wanted to spend my life with him."

Casey ignored Maureen's comment but must have realized she was gaping again. She closed her mouth with a snap. "That's it? True? That's all you can say? For crying out loud, you live in Boston!"

Kyra lost her smile. She touched her sister's shoulder. "I swore if I got you back alive I'd make changes in my life. Even if I hadn't fallen in love with Lucan, I'd already decided to move here to be closer to you. Casey, your kids didn't even know me. We're family and I've been woefully neglectful of that. But I want a chance for us to be closer. I already love your children. I want to be part of their lives. You know, the wacky aunt who buys them presents and spoils them rotten? E-mails and phone calls aren't enough."

"You're serious."

"Absolutely."

Casey shook her head. "What about your job?"

"I can get another job."

"Not doing the sort of work you've been doing."

She shrugged. "It's time for a change there as well. I'm tired of all the traveling. I have an apartment I never see. I want a home and maybe someday a family of my own."

"I don't know what to say."

"How about welcome to the neighborhood?" Kyra smiled again. "And if either of you happen to know of anyone looking to hire a lawyer with international law and insurance work in their background…"

She hugged her sister close. "It's going to be okay. I promise, Casey. No matter what happens with Lucan, I'm here to stay. Did you bring me a change of clothing?" she asked Maureen.

"Your bag is on the floor behind the driver's side."

"You're really going to stay here?" Casey demanded.

"Well, it's getting a bit crowded at Maureen's, wouldn't you say? As long as you're okay with this." She looked at the older woman.

"Lucan's a grown man, an' yer both old enough to know your own minds." Maureen's smile lit her face once more. "Welcome to the neighborhood."

Kyra was still smiling as she retrieved her suitcase. But a van coming down the street started to drive past and slowed. The driver gaped at her. He braked hard, throwing his passenger against the seatbelt. Kyra didn't wait to see more. There was a scar on the driver's left cheek. She fled back into the house.

"The men who shot at me are outside! We have to run!"

"I can't run on this knee, Kyra!" Casey crossed to the fireplace and hefted a poker. "But I'm pretty good with a baseball bat. This should make a fair substitute."

"They have guns!"

"So did Lucan."

Maureen ran to the kitchen and returned holding a heavy metal skillet, a can of oven spray and a portable phone. She thrust the can at Kyra as she pressed 911. "'Tis not that pepper spray stuff ye used, but 't'will burn the eyes just the same. We need the police," she said into the phone. "Two killers are breaking into our house."

And they were out of time and out of choices. The men were running up onto the porch.

Casey took a stand on the far side of the door. The poker was clutched in her good right hand. Maureen dropped the phone and moved alongside her holding the skillet. There was nothing else to be done. Kyra stood facing the door. She pointed the container of oven spray and prayed for a miracle.

The door flew inward on the second kick. Casey swung the poker with all her might as the first man rushed inside. The crunch sounded unnaturally loud. The man yelled as she hit him again and he went sprawling. His gun discharged harmlessly into the wall over the fireplace.

Maureen brought the pan down on the second man's head with a dull, thunking sound while Kyra leaped forward, spraying the oven cleaner directly into his face.

He flinched away. That was his mistake. Casey swung the poker once again. The pointed, slightly hooked end struck his gun hand. Kyra heard bones crunch as he screamed, shrill and loud. The gun fell from useless fingers.

Maureen had picked up the first man's gun. As the second man turned on Casey, she fired. The man staggered, blood staining his thigh.

Kyra dropped the can of oven cleaner and picked up the frying pan. When he lunged forward at Maureen, she hit him across the back with enough force to send him down beside his friend.

Abruptly, the air was filled with sirens. Uniformed police officers converged on the porch with guns drawn.

Casey stood over the conscious man, brandishing the poker. "Never mess with a Wolfstead."

"Or an O'Shay," Maureen put in.

Chapter Sixteen

"'T'was the night before Christmas and all through the house…"

Kyra stood in the dining room of Maureen's house, near the kitchen. Neil was giving a dramatic reading to the cluster of adults and children crowded inside his mother's living room. It was three days until Christmas. Lucan had been called into work once more. He'd missed dinner again, but Kyra was keeping a plate warm for him in the oven.

She never heard the kitchen door open, but she felt the cold draft on her back and whirled around. Lucan motioned her to silence and gestured for her to join him. Kyra knew Phyllis had noticed, but the woman didn't make a sound as they hurried out the back door.

"What is it? What's wrong now?" Kyra whispered, shivering in the cold.

"Nothing. But it's been hours since I've had you alone long enough to do this."

She came into his arms, kissing him back with equal fervor until her legs turned to liquid. "We're going to shock your mother's neighbors," she whispered breathlessly.

"Hmm. Serves them right for being nosy. What would you say to going back to my house and getting naked?"

"I thought you'd never ask."

He grinned. "Let's go."

"I need my coat. It's freezing out here."

"You can wear mine. The car is warm and if we go back inside we'll never get out of there."

"I need to let your mother and my sister know we're leaving."

"You could call them later."

She poked him in the chest. "We aren't randy teenagers, for heaven's sake."

"No, we're randy adults."

The back door opened. Kip stepped outside holding out Kyra's purse and coat. "His mom said 'You don't want to be leavin' your purse an' coat.' Oh, and you should take the plate of food warming in the oven."

Lucan grinned. Kyra was thankful it was too dark for Kip to see her blushing.

"Thanks, sport," Lucan told him. "Do me a favor and turn off the oven. I'm going to eat when I get home."

Kyra poked him hard in the ribs before putting on her coat.

"Lucan?" Kip asked seriously, "Did that man your mom shot die?"

He released Kyra to face the boy. "No, Kip. He's out of danger now. Both men are going to live to stand trial for kidnapping your mother, and trying to kill her and your aunt and my mother. They also have to answer for murdering a woman whose home they broke into. At the very least, those men are going to go to jail for a very long time."

"That's good. Thanks, Lucan. You know, for finding my mom and everything. Aunt Kyra said you would, and you did."

"It's my job, Kip."

"I know. I'm going to be a detective when I grow up, too."

He ruffled the boy's hair. "Get inside before you freeze."

"Okay. 'Night, Aunt Kyra."

"Good night, honey."

Kyra shook her head at Lucan the moment Kip disappeared. "Now see what you've done? He wants to be a cop when he grows up."

"And what's wrong with that? He might have wanted to be a lawyer."

"You are going to pay for that crack, Detective," she warned, sliding into his newest unmarked police car.

"I'm counting on it." He waggled his eyebrows suggestively, closed the door and went around to the driver's side.

"Is Montgomery really going to be okay?" she asked.

Lucan started the engine and pulled out onto the street. "Yep. And Robby Krinegolt is talking, hoping for leniency. White or Fillmont or whatever you want to call him got together with Montgomery over some beers one night. Montgomery mentioned his friend, Paul Atteril, operated a string of pawn shops in the Baltimore area. So White came up with the idea of using the club as a source of information on some of their wealthier clientele. Both men were in a good position to chat up members of the club about vacation and travel plans, and it dawned on them that as a waiter and errand boy, Krinegolt heard even more. Krinegolt kept complaining he needed cash to move out of his mother's place. White had the know-how, Montgomery had access to addresses and private information, and Krinegolt owned a van and lived in a basement where he could store whatever they needed."

"So they teamed up."

Lucan nodded. "They were careful to strike only when no one would be home. Until Shereen Nestler made the fateful mistake of changing her plans at the last minute. Krinegolt swears it was Montgomery she surprised."

"And he says it was Krinegolt?"

Lucan shook his head. "Nope. He claims it was White.

White's dead, so it's Montgomery's word against Krinegolt's. I'm inclined to believe Krinegolt. Robby says she started screaming so Montgomery began choking her to shut her up. When she went limp, he panicked and threw her down against the coffee table. White was in another part of the house. Krinegolt says she was dead when he got there."

"Jordan stole the necklace off her dead body?"

"Actually, her necklace had broken in the struggle. White ordered them to finish loading the van, picked up the pendant and took the ring off her finger. No doubt he would have taken her earrings as well, but Montgomery and Krinegolt were in a panic to leave. They'd started to suspect he was holding out cash on them, but they didn't know he took the woman's pendant and ring until it made the news. They were furious. They knew the jewelry would tie them to the murder. White insisted he had them someplace safe and knew a jeweler who would break them down and get them a good price."

"But they didn't trust him anymore, so he ran."

Lucan shook his head. "No, that's where things got complicated. They were upset with White, but they still had two more robberies planned. They went ahead with the Fisk job and were set to go again when White stared out the window that fateful Sunday. Bill Jaff, the golf pro, was showing a man around. White recognized him immediately as an enforcer for the man White had sent to prison."

"A contract killer?" she yelped.

"Well, we'd never be able to prove it, but essentially, yes. White fled and called Casey to warn her."

"Nice of him."

"Yeah. He didn't know Montgomery and Krinegolt were off that day and had decided to go to your sister's house to recover the ring and the pendant. They wanted to destroy them and get the money they were sure White was holding out on them."

"But Casey didn't know what they were talking about. Why didn't she recognize them?"

"They were wearing ski masks. She'd barely met either of them if you'll recall. When they didn't have any luck finding the stuff they decided to hold her until White gave them what they wanted. They were driving a car Krinegolt had stolen so no one would be able to ID them from the license plate."

"The car my sister wrecked."

"Exactly. Montgomery knew one of the club members owned a furnished rental unit that was standing empty, so they took your sister there."

"She escaped and the contract killer wanted to use Casey the same way. But he thought I was her."

Lucan nodded. "When you got away at the shopping center, we think he decided to hole up in Casey and Jordan's house. He figured one of them would show back up sooner or later."

"Which I did. My sister has deplorable taste in men."

He pulled into his driveway. "She seems to be wondering about your taste as well."

"My taste is impeccable."

He grinned. "No argument here."

Lucan seemed nervous as he led her up to the front porch and unlocked the door. She put it down to anticipation, which only heightened her own.

The scent of pine hit her the moment he opened the door. He hit the light switch as she stepped inside. Instead of the floor lamps, a softly glowing Christmas tree came to life.

"Lucan! When did you do this?"

"Tonight. Todd helped me. That's why I was so late. I know how much you enjoy sitting by Mom's tree. The thing is, I don't have much in the way of ornaments. I thought maybe you could help me shop for some."

Pleasure flooded her. "You even decorated the bookcase!"

Greenery and red candles adorned the shelves. Two red

stockings hung to either side of the fireplace opening. The tree itself was bedecked with what looked like a million twinkling lights and tiny red bows. A white angel perched precariously on the topmost branch of the slightly crooked tree, its fiber optic wings changing color.

"You did this for me?"

"Do you like it?"

"No, I don't like it, I love it! Thank you, thank you, thank you!" Tears stung her eyes. She closed them so he wouldn't see. She couldn't believe how much crying she'd done since coming here, even if these were tears of joy for a change.

"Hey. Are you crying?"

She sniffed. "Not yet." She opened her eyes to find him smiling with such utter tenderness she thought her heart might burst with happiness. Until she saw his serious expression. "What's wrong?"

"Nothing's wrong. Kyra, I'm a cop."

"I know." Fear nested in the pit of her stomach.

"My mother, your sister and my sister-in-law are already planning our wedding."

Somehow, Kyra kept her expression neutral.

"I don't work a nine-to-five job. I see and deal with the things most people only read about. Sometimes what I see is hard to leave behind when I'm off the clock. Cops miss dance recitals and little league games. We work through holidays and birthdays. That sort of thing takes a toll on relationships."

"This is sounding an awful lot like an 'it's been fun, but' speech."

"No!"

'Good, 'cause it needs work.'

He ran a hand through his hair. His features were strained. "I've got one failed marriage already. You need to understand—"

"That loving a cop is hard work?" She closed the distance

between them and aimed her index finger at his face. "I've got news for you, O'Shay, loving anyone is hard work. Think you've seen me at my worst? Wait for a bad day." She jabbed the finger in his chest. "You love me. Say it."

The tension ebbed from his body. "I thought I had." He nodded to the room.

"Not good enough, O'Shay."

He clasped her upper arms. "Words are easy."

"But important."

"Yeah. Yes, they are. I love you, Kyra."

Her heart hitched in relief. "That wasn't so hard, was it?"

"Not hard at all." And he claimed her mouth the way he'd claimed her heart.

They finally came up for air and she gazed around the room, at the love he'd put into decorating it for her. "I love you, Lucan."

"That being the case…" His smile was achingly tender. "I'd get down on my knees, but I'm afraid I might spoil it and not be able to get up again. There wasn't time to pick out a ring, but I was wondering if you'd consider marrying me."

Her heart sang. "Already did that. The answer is yes."

"I'll give you time…"

She shook her head and pulled his down for another quick kiss. "I don't need time, Lucan."

The tenderness of his smile made it hard to breathe. "Then how would you feel about eloping?"

Laughter welled in her chest. "And deprive our families of a wedding extravaganza?"

Lucan heaved a mock smile. "It was worth a shot."

She wound her arms around his neck. "I'll take you any way I can get you, Lucan O'Shay. Bring on the justice of the peace if that's what you want. But *you* have to tell your mother."

"No thanks, I'm not that brave. Oh well, Maggie will make an adorable flower girl." He clasped the side of her face. "I love you, Kyra."

"I love you, too. Shall we head upstairs?"

He laughed. "Why waste time? We've got a couch, a rug and a Christmas tree."

"Fine, but it's your turn to be on the bottom."

"Race you upstairs?"

Bestselling author Lynne Graham is back with a fabulous new trilogy!

PREGNANT BRIDES

Three ordinary girls—naive, but also honest and plucky...

Three fabulously wealthy, impossibly handsome and very ruthless men...

When opposites attract and passion leads to pregnancy... it can only mean marriage!

Available next month from Harlequin Presents®: the first installment

DESERT PRINCE, BRIDE OF INNOCENCE

* * *

'THIS EVENING I'm flying to New York for two weeks,' Jasim imparted with a casualness that made her heart sink like a stone. 'That's why I had you brought here. I own this apartment and you'll be comfortable here while I'm abroad.'

'I can afford my own accommodation although I may not need it for long. I'll have another job by the time you get back—'

Jasim released a slightly harsh laugh. 'There's no need for you to look for another position. How would I ever see you? Don't you understand what I'm offering you?'

Elinor stood very still. 'No, I must be incredibly thick because I haven't quite worked out yet what you're offering me....'

His charismatic smile slashed his lean dark visage. 'Naturally, I want to take care of you....'

'No, thanks.' Elinor forced a smile and mentally willed him not to demean her with some sordid proposition. 'The only man who will ever take *care* of me with my agreement will be my husband. I'm willing to wait for you to come back but I'm not willing to be kept by you. I'm a very independent woman and what I give, I give freely.'

Jasim frowned. 'You make it all sound so serious.'

'What happened between us last night left pure chaos in its wake. Right now, I don't know whether I'm on my head or my heels. I'll stay for a while because I have nowhere else to go in the short term. So maybe it's good that you'll be away for a while.'

Jasim pulled out his wallet to extract a card. 'My private number,' he told her, presenting her with it as though it was a precious gift, which indeed it was. Many women would have done just about anything to gain access to that direct hotline to him, but his staff guarded his privacy with scrupulous care.

Before he could close the wallet, his blood ran cold in his veins. How could he have made such a serious oversight? What if he had got her pregnant? He knew that an unplanned pregnancy would engulf his life like an avalanche, crush his freedom and suffocate him. He barely stilled a shudder at the threat of such an outcome and thought how ironic it was that what his older brother had longed and prayed for to secure the line to the throne should strike Jasim as an absolute disaster....

* * *

What will proud Prince Jasim do if Elinor is expecting his royal baby? Perhaps an arranged marriage is the only solution! But will Elinor agree? Find out in DESERT PRINCE, BRIDE OF INNOCENCE by Lynne Graham [#2884], available from Harlequin Presents® in January 2010.

HARLEQUIN *Presents*

Bestselling Harlequin Presents author

Lynne Graham

brings you an exciting new miniseries:

PREGNANT BRIDES

Inexperienced and expecting, they're forced to marry

Collect them all:

DESERT PRINCE, BRIDE OF INNOCENCE

January 2010

RUTHLESS MAGNATE, CONVENIENT WIFE

February 2010

GREEK TYCOON, INEXPERIENCED MISTRESS

March 2010

REQUEST YOUR FREE BOOKS!

2 FREE NOVELS PLUS 2 FREE GIFTS!

HARLEQUIN®

INTRIGUE®

Breathtaking Romantic Suspense

YES! Please send me 2 FREE Harlequin Intrigue® novels and my 2 FREE gifts (gifts are worth about $10). After receiving them, if I don't wish to receive any more books, I can return the shipping statement marked "cancel." If I don't cancel, I will receive 6 brand-new novels every month and be billed just $4.24 per book in the U.S. or $4.99 per book in Canada. That's a savings of close to 15% off the cover price! It's quite a bargain! Shipping and handling is just 50¢ per book.* I understand that accepting the 2 free books and gifts places me under no obligation to buy anything. I can always return a shipment and cancel at any time. Even if I never buy another book from Harlequin, the two free books and gifts are mine to keep forever.

182 HDN EYTR   382 HDN EYT3

Name	(PLEASE PRINT)	
Address		Apt. #
City	State/Prov.	Zip/Postal Code

Signature (if under 18, a parent or guardian must sign)

Mail to the **Harlequin Reader Service**:
IN U.S.A.: P.O. Box 1867, Buffalo, NY 14240-1867
IN CANADA: P.O. Box 609, Fort Erie, Ontario L2A 5X3

Not valid to current subscribers of Harlequin Intrigue books.

**Are you a current subscriber of Harlequin Intrigue books
and want to receive the larger-print edition?
Call 1-800-873-8635 today!**

* Terms and prices subject to change without notice. Prices do not include applicable taxes. Sales tax applicable in N.Y. Canadian residents will be charged applicable provincial taxes and GST. Offer not valid in Quebec. This offer is limited to one order per household. All orders subject to approval. Credit or debit balances in a customer's account(s) may be offset by any other outstanding balance owed by or to the customer. Please allow 4 to 6 weeks for delivery. Offer available while quantities last.

Your Privacy: Harlequin is committed to protecting your privacy. Our Privacy Policy is available online at www.eHarlequin.com or upon request from the Reader Service. From time to time we make our lists of customers available to reputable third parties who may have a product or service of interest to you. If you would prefer we not share your name and address, please check here. ☐

HI09R

HARLEQUIN® *Blaze*™

New Year, New Man!

*For the perfect New Year's punch,
blend the following:*

- *One woman determined to find her inner vixen*
- *A notorious—and notoriously hot!—playboy*
- *A provocative New Year's Eve bash*
- *An impulsive kiss that leads to a night of explosive passion!*

When the clock hits midnight Claire Daniels
kisses the guy standing closest to her, but
the kiss doesn't end after the bells stop ringing....

Look for

Moonstruck

by *USA TODAY* bestselling author

JULIE KENNER

Available January

---

red-hot reads

www.eHarlequin.com

HB79518

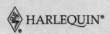

HARLEQUIN®

INTRIGUE®

COMING NEXT MONTH

Available January 12, 2010

#1179 THE SOCIALITE AND THE BODYGUARD
by Dana Marton
Bodyguard of the Month
The ex-commando bodyguard couldn't believe his luck when he was assigned to protect a socialite's poodle. But as he learns that opposites really can attract, he also realizes that his socialite may be the real target of the death threats....

#1180 CLASSIFIED COWBOY by Mallory Kane
The Silver Star of Texas: Comanche Creek
The forensic anthropologist had caught the Texas Ranger's eye years ago, and now he's back for a second chance at love—and at cracking an old case.

#1181 THE SHADOW by Aimée Thurlo
Brotherhood of Warriors
After a series of incidents and threats puts her project—and her life—in jeopardy, she has no choice but to depend on the ex-army ranger to protect her.

#1182 A PERFECT STRANGER by Jenna Ryan
On the run, her new life is put in danger when a gorgeous ex-cop tracks her down and unknowingly exposes her. His conscience won't let him abandon her, and their attraction can only grow stronger... if they survive.

#1183 CASE FILE: CANYON CREEK, WYOMING
by Paula Graves
Cooper Justice
After almost falling victim to a killer, she's the only one who can help a determined Wyoming officer bring him to justice.

#1184 THE SHERIFF OF SILVERHILL by Carol Ericson
The FBI agent returns home to investigate a serial killer, only to find that the sheriff she's working with is the man she had to leave behind.

www.eHarlequin.com

HICNMBPA1209